# The Carter Chronicles

Louis Combe

*In the beginning, the Great Mystery Power used loving and caring to cre-ate Mother Earth and all the People. The ending was made the same time as the beginning, so all paths exist for the return. The Great-Grandmother watches over the Hohokum People. She will reveal the true path to the return if they have strong hearts.*

—Hohokum Cosmology

*May you be happy,*
*May you be safe,*
*May you be peaceful,*
*May you have ease*
*of well-being.*

—Buddhist Loving Kindness Meditation

*So many gods, so many creeds,*
*So many paths that wind and wind,*
*When just the art of being kind*
*Is all the sad world needs.*

—Ella Wheeler Wilcox (1850-1919)

*For my wife, Bettie Carter Combe*
*For my son, Kirk Clayton Combe*

# Prologue

Sarah, the only, lonely child of an abusive mother and a malleable father, was never granted loving and caring at the house where she lived. For reasons not explained to her, Sarah was at fault. She longed for – and envied – the loving and caring others enjoyed at their houses.

During her grade school years, Sarah decided that she was given to the wrong people, in the wrong place, and for the wrong reasons. Did the stork leave her atop the wrong chimney? Or had the gypsies stolen her from a place of loving and caring and brought her to the far western United States for gold? Sarah never felt at home with the home life she was forced to live, but she had no other path to follow. She secretly longed to be bold and assertive, so that she could oppose her so-called mother, who denied her the loving and caring of her timid father.

In her high school years, Sarah decided that the Carter couple she lived with were themselves at fault and incapable of giving her the loving and caring she deserved. One of her grandmothers – the always-angry one – lived nearby. She was Sarah's only confidant and confessed similar suspicions of displacement when she was a youngster, before her girlish longings were overwhelmed by the harsh realities for females in the closed, male dominated community where they lived. She told Sarah that her mother – Sarah's great-grandmother – was filled with lifelong rage because the great, mysterious power that decided her life's path had sent her to the wrong place for the wrong reasons. Sarah's great-grandmother fought in vain to escape the outrages she suffered and return to her rightful place in a far away household filled with loving and caring.

Sarah's other grandmother was a docile follower of the dead-end path dictated to her by the males. The docile grandmother chided the angry grandmother for her blasphemies and died gladly, eager for the rewards promised by the males in an afterlife they continued to dominate. Was Sarah doomed to remain a docile follower also?

Sarah found a glimmer of hope in her great-grandmother's contention that a great mystery power had made a miscalculation and decided that she, too, was a Carter placed on the wrong path. Such fanciful musings served to strengthen Sarah's sense of displacement. How did she actually get shunted off on the wrong branch of the Carter family tree? How could she find the path back to the Carters who would give her the loving and caring she deserved?

Determined to discover the roots of her true Carter ancestry, Sarah majored in English history at a local university, hoping that she could detect when, where, why, and how her rightful path had been detoured. By the time she graduated, Sarah had acquired considerable knowledge but no understanding of the complex factors leading to her predicament.

Evidently, carters, the folks that haul all sorts of things in carts, had been part of a six-thousand-year migration of peoples – including those now known as Anglo-Saxons – from more than halfway around the earth. Being at the ending point of this astounding migration, Sarah pledged to employ all her energies and meager resources to retrace her path back to the source of her true ancestry. As her fisherman father would say, she would be a salmon swimming upstream in history to the source of her beginning. Sarah decided to construct a chronological record of events, a Carter Chronicles.

The Great Mystery Power finally favored Sarah when national attention focused on the Carter Roadways Company as she was searching for job opportunities. The dynamic company president, Grethe Carter, had recently relocated the large, rapidly expanding road construction company to Chapel Hill, North Carolina. Stories in national newspapers informed Sarah that Grethe was the third generation of Carter females to lead Roadways. Did this Carter female represent Sarah's rightful clan? Surely, Grethe had dominated her opponents with bold determination and readiness for conflict, a model of assertiveness.

Sarah launched her reverse migration by journeying to Chapel Hill and securing employment as a high school history teacher. Not daring to approach Grethe with her bizarre mission to delve into her past, Sarah searched for the means to discover if Grethe held the key to her rightful path to loving and caring.

# The Carter Chronicles

## Chronicler
## Sarah Chamberlain

In the Beginning wandering tribes of Angles and Saxon horsemen journeyed ever westward from Central Asia in pursuit of plunder in greener pastures. Mounted warriors in the vanguard led the host, first to engage all in their paths with sword, battleaxe, and lance, and first to confiscate the property of those defeated. These assertive warrior leaders were fired with bold determination and readiness for conflict. They dominated crises of their own creation by rising above the fray on their horses, identifying crucial elements, and controlling their actions. They risked everything to win everything.

Laws for acquiring, holding, and transferring property were fiercely enforced. Primogeniture – the exclusive right of inheritance by the eldest son – prevailed in each clan. If all males in a clan died, a daughter was captured and raped by a rival clansman and declared a bride. Thus, the property passed. Might and expediency made right.

Carters performed the cartage of the property to the next conquest. Following the mounted vanguard in the dust and the offal, they tugged and pushed their crude wheeled creations. Spent warhorses and commandeered oxen were at times allocated to the carters to hasten the warrior elites' pursuit of riches. Carters and other followers survived by attaching themselves to the leaders for protection. They risked little and received little.

Warrior clan females – as well as carter females – were subject to bride-capture violations throughout the centuries-long trek. At Europe's lands end the Angles and the Saxons ferried their property – and bride-capture laws – to the big island called Albion – later Britain – their westward surge seemingly spent save for Ireland Isle.

536 ...........................................................................

The Anglo-Saxon chieftains were in constant battles for the property of the inhabitants of the big and small islands, and then battled among themselves. Carters were lowly serfs, but uniquely due the cartbote – wood due them from the forests controlled by the chieftains – to build carts. Blacksmiths and carpenters assisted in the fashioning and repair of their wheeled vehicles. A hardy group of carters congregated at Oxford Village where their oxen forded the Thames River pulling high-wheeled carts.

899 ...........................................................................

King Alfred, the great defender of Wessex, died. He relied on the carters for the cartage of his goods throughout Wessex, as well as the repair of Roman roadways and bridges with the aid of masons and carpenters. Carters were also essential to the construction of earth and stone burrhs, the crude fortifications erected to defend against the Danes. An excellent burrh was built around Oxford.

1066 ...........................................................................

William of Normandy, aided by the French legions, conquered King Harold at Hastings. Harold risked dismounting his warhorse and lost all of England. Warrior Earl Ethelred, carrying the royal Dragon of Wessex standard, died when he also dismounted from his warhorse to stand by the last Anglo-Saxon king. Forevermore, Harold is the name of a fool. Carters later entered the field of battle to collect with loving care the Anglo-Saxon dead. They then pilfered the purses of the despicable French and left their carcasses to rot. Sarah longed to be descended from the bold, assertive, and loyal Wessex.

1553    ...............................................................................

Duke Cedric of Wessex, the renowned warrior-scholar, was killed during civil unrest at Oxford. He was waylaid while inadvertently taking the wrong path from the armory to the lecture hall. Harold the Rotund Mason kidnapped and raped Flossie, a young, unmarried heiress from a rival mason clan, when her men folks were killed during these troubles. Civil and church blessings were bestowed on this lawful bride capture that enlarged the master mason's construction cartel.

1588    ...............................................................................

A Spanish Armada of one hundred and fifty ships set sail against Britain. The Hispanics were bent on punishing the Anglo-Saxons for raids on their empire in the Americas upon which their wealth and military might depended. Good fortune, foul weather, and the derring-do of privately owned vessels eliminated the threat of the large fleet. Captain Morgan Wessex, newly returned from privateer raids on Hispanic gold-bearing ships off the coasts of the Americas, further distinguished the Wessex Dragon standard. Carters teamed with stevedores at the Oxford wharves to fetch the plunder to the nearby Wessex fortified country house.

**1597** ....................................................................

George the Carter of Oxford added the repair of carts to his cartage craft. When he died without male issue, Balder the Blacksmith directed his eldest son, Jerric, to violate George's fourteen-year-old daughter, Ludie, and lay claim to the property. Bessie the Barmaid, Ludie's mother, was sent to the poor house. This bride-capture was aborted when Jerric died from poison mushrooms in his stew. Ludie managed the carter enterprise until Wayne, the son conceived of Jerric's rape, reached his majority. Ultimately, Ludie was burned at the stake as a witch. Churchmen hated and feared competent women. Ludie Carter was the taproot of Grethe's family tree.

**1653** ....................................................................

Bride-capture was recognized as an economic opportunity to the British crown, so a law was passed that gave the ruling nobility one-half the loot a male gained from raping a female for her property. Thereafter, bride-capture was less blatant to avoid taxes; but the pain, shame, and property losses to females were not diminished. Anglo-Saxon females traveled a vast distance from Central Asia to an ultimate homeland, but male bride-capture mentalities remained long after justifications for this expediency existed. Unbridled might makes greed and corruption.

**1776** ....................................................................

Anglo-Saxon wanderlust in pursuit of expansion of their empire drew warrior-leaders and a host of underclass followers westward to the Americas where tax disputes created breakaway colonies sandwiched between the Hispanics and the French. In this land where several states united, distinctions between leaders and followers –

warriors and carters and their ilk — were frequently blurred, causing role confusion among those newly entering the vast lands waiting to be conquered. Sarah uses "Anglo-Saxon" instead of "British" or "English" to stress the Anglo-Saxons' particular unremitting pursuit of property in battle or in business.

1840 .........................................................................

Thomas Carter loved to speed the carts, so he establishing a rapid cartage business throughout Oxford's outskirts. Young Chester Carpenter, jealous of innovation, took over this carter initiative by murdering Thomas and marrying his widow, Amber, who was twenty years Chester's senior. Amber made rapid, vigorous recovery from her bride-capture ordeal. Sarah's docile grandmother was descended from Thomas's clan which was separate from Grethe's family tree, so, regretfully, one of Sarah's ancestors was a follower who risked little and received nothing.

1870 .........................................................................

The remainder of the nineteenth century brought revolutionary industrial change and the need for carters to reinvent themselves as railroads reduced their ranks. Many pursued the building of carriages and wagons. The Oxford carters increasingly employed themselves in the construction and repair of roadways and bridges.

1877 .........................................................................

Anglo-Saxon warriors' treks throughout the far-flung British empire created a population imbalance with females of marriageable age more numerous than males. Females without property and marriage prospects journeyed to the new lands in the United States of America where males outnumbered females. Many carter females — and others considered to be the low-born — emigrated and sought menial positions in east coast cities. Ethel Wessex, a maiden longing for loving and caring, emigrated also, but she trekked westward. False male prophets lured her to the far west with promises of an Avalon — a golden land of milk and honey. But Ethel, a Wessex, was forced to be a carter, delivering herself to her own bride-capture by tugging a handcart to a land of salt, sexual degradation, and female despair. Ethel's bride-capture resulted in her becoming plural property of a male charlatan with bizarre pretensions of sainthood. Ethel was Sarah's outraged great-grandmother.

1882      ..................................................................

The Carter Roadways Company in Oxford prospered, so many competitors coveted it. Mariah was born to Albert and Idella Cook Carter, who died birthing Mariah. Ruth, the wise nursemaid, prophesied that this female child would achieve greatness. Mariah was a precocious child, an early, avid reader of books and quick to learn her numbers. Aided by her doting father, she understood that her twin liabilities — a carter and a female — would prevent her from practicing male assertive leadership methods.

1898      ..................................................................

Rejecting the option of being dominated by a male, Mariah searched for alternatives. She determined that the decline in internal armed conflict among the Anglo-Saxon clans led to the increasing use of cunningness as an acceptable male leadership mode. Increasingly, crafty males became highly skilled in acquiring the property of others by devious means. Opponents were influenced through shrewd and subtly resourceful means, so that desired outcomes were achieved without the males encountering direct conflict. Mariah concluded that cunning leadership was an acquired proficiency so that no male, strong-armed hulks on horses were required. Cunningness could be a means for leadership equal opportunity for females. Mariah was Grethe's grandmother directly descended from Ludie, who appears in the Chronicles in 1597.

1900        ........................................................................

Willis Clayton, of the Chester carters, was married to Mariah as encouraged by Albert on his deathbed. Willis promptly violated promises made to Albert and confiscated all of Mariah's assets and moved to Philadelphia in the United States of America to join the Anglo-Saxons' continued westward migration. Mariah avoided direct confrontations with Willis, but she was ever alert for opportunities to escape the follower role relegated to her.

1910        ........................................................................

Carriages were being made obsolete by the mass production of motorized carts. Many carters became the drivers of these oxen-less vehicles. The Clayton Carriage Company struggled in Pennsylvania until Willis died of a brain seizure. Mariah reclaimed her maiden Carter name, and, while caring for her six-year-old daughter Lisbeth, fended off creditors and ambitious suitors and made a success of her newly chartered Carter Roadways Company, solely dedicated to the construction of roads and bridges. Lisbeth grew up in Roadways' headquarters that afforded a view of the Philadelphia Museum of Art and the then-pristine Schuykill River. She received the maximum higher education available to females and intensive tutoring from Mariah on the art of leading Roadways through the practice of cunning leadership.

1920 ...............................................................

Females were given the right to vote. Mariah's company charter provided that only Carter females could lead Roadways, much to the amusement of local male power brokers. Females hailed Mariah's initiative as a sign of great progress, but secretly believed this suffrage initiative was doomed to failure. Mariah instructed Lisbeth to devise a groom-capture beneficial to Roadways by marrying a malleable man susceptible to being shaped to her needs and owning property that would expand Roadways. She was to deny him power and retain the Carter name. Mariah assured Lisbeth that pursuing this canny path would protect against future bride-capture of Carter females.

1940 ...............................................................

After Mariah's death, Lisbeth married Chester Carpenter, owner of a company constructing wooden bridges in rural areas. Chester belatedly learned that Lisbeth would retain the Carter name and the Roadways presidency. Lisbeth soon incorporated all of the Carpenter Company assets under the Roadways' banner, permitting Chester to dabble at bridge construction in Mexico near his favored marlin fishing haunts. Chester sired two sons, Fred and Hack, and ridiculed the "great Mariah's" edict of female domination of Roadways.

1945

Grethe Carter was born and Chester was relegated to a being full-time builder of bridges and roads in Mexico. He ended his days as a disgruntled, debauched consort, but developed worthwhile assets in Mexico by allying himself with Don Carlos Emblema and his Emblema Compañia headquartered in Mexico City. After completing her education agenda, Grethe received increasingly more responsible management assignments from Lisbeth. Fred and Hack plotted her eventual downfall between fishing trips in Mexico.

1960

Lisbeth hired Josiah Chamberlain, an assertive, young road construction superintendent, to oversee Mexican construction projects, because projects were plentiful but not profitable, a crisis in Lisbeth's estimation. Profit performance improved rapidly, so Lisbeth continued joint road construction projects with Don Carlos.

1964

Females were included in the Civil Rights Act. Lisbeth died and Fred and Hack strived to void Mariah's doctrine of female leadership of Roadways. Grethe accomplished another successful groom-capture by marrying the most malleable Walter "Buck" Smith in Chapel Hill, North Carolina, her Anglo-Saxon western expansion veering southward. She left an aging headquarters building, and little else, to her brothers. The Smith Fleet Maintenance Company was integrated with Roadways. A new headquarters building and a nearby residence were constructed in Chapel Hill. Roadways then took full advantage of the highway construction boom underway throughout the United States.

1968          ...................................................................

Sarah married Josiah Chamberlain, accomplishing a
groom-capture facilitating her reverse migration from the
far west. Fearing that she was too old to benefit from the
equal employment opportunities promised females, she
joined Josiah on his nomadic career path. Two sons, Josh
and Noah, completed their family circle. Sarah home-
schooled her sons at several Mexican road construction
sites and continued her scholarly pursuits as well as she
could, harboring an intense desire to earn a doctorate
degree in English history to enable her to chronicle the
Carters.

1970          ...................................................................

Ludie Carter was born to Grethe. Insiders considered it a
minor miracle birth in that Buck now spent the vast
majority of his time in Monte Carlo and the international
race car circuit. From an early age, Ludie was taught her
great-grandmother Mariah's guiding principles for cunning leadership. Grethe limited Buck's access to Ludie.

1973          ...................................................................

Don Carlos presented Grethe a joint venture proposition
outside the Roadways charter that she could not refuse –
partnership in a rich gold deposit within a high mesa in
Sonora, Mexico. Don Carlos dubbed the mine Cíbola,
the mythical Spanish city of gold. Grethe directed Josiah
to construct and operate an open pit gold mine and ore
processing facility. Sarah, Noah, and Josh accompanied
Josiah on this assignment for the next five years. To
Sarah's delight and gratitude, she discovered that Josh
and Noah – her two perfect sons – ended her search for
loving and caring. The unconditional love that they

shared with her far exceeded her fondest dreams. Sarah shed her pain and sorrow during five golden years at Cíbola. The Great Mystery Power had made amends for past miscalculations, but she remained determined to discover the full truths of her ancestry.

1978 ......................................................................

The Chamberlains moved to major road construction projects throughout Latin America. Josiah gloried in his increasing skills as an assertive crisis intervention specialist serving the needs of Grethe and Roadways.

1984 ......................................................................

Josiah was promoted to Roadways' Managing Director, necessitating his extensive travels throughout the world. Grethe relied on his assertive leadership capabilities to preserve her cunning posture. Then, the virulent forces of primogeniture shaped Josh's relationships with Sarah and Noah. He decided to follow Josiah's big business career path and enrolled in a northern university. Josh withdrew from Sarah's orbit, to her lasting sorrow. Sarah and Noah lived in a condominium in Chapel Hill. Sarah returned to teaching at a Chapel Hill high school, while Noah attended high school and enrolled at the University of North Carolina.

1988 ......................................................................

Sarah learned that Grethe's ancestors migrated from Oxford Village in England, so she enrolled in an English history doctoral program each summer at Oxford University. Josh graduated and joined a rival construction company. Noah dated Ludie during his senior year in high school. But Grethe ordered Josiah to instruct Noah to end his relationship with Ludie, threatening dismissal if he refused. Josiah, always the faithful Chamberlain, complied. Sarah was elated when Ludie and Noah were separated. She didn't raise her malleable son to be fodder for the Carter maneaters.

1992

Noah graduated from UNC with a B.A. in social studies. Rejecting Roadways' employment offer, he taught English to Spanish-speaking children in Barcelona during the Olympics and lingered in Spain working for a bilingual Spanish-English school, happy to escape Josiah's orbit. Sarah suffered greatly from her separation from Noah, fearing the loss of a second son who represented loving and caring to her.

1994

The United States business community touted the North American Free Trade Agreement – NAFTA – free trade legislation as a win-win situation for all, but wage earners across all borders feared lose-lose conditions for them. Don Carlos urged Grethe to increase his powers in their partnership, but she refused because this would reduce Roadways' profits. After graduating from Duke University, Ludie feigned interest in racecars to gain access to Buck. Grethe feared that Ludie was not qualified for her future role as Roadways' President.

1996

Don Carlos died and his oldest son, Carlos IV, succeeded him as President of Emblema Compañia. Ludie and Buck attended Don Carlos' funeral in Mexico City, and then accepted Carlos IV's younger brother Victor's invitation to participate in a Lower Baja road rally. Grethe directed Josiah to fetch Ludie back from the Puerta Vallarta extended victory celebration.

1997

Grethe decided to expand Roadways' construction opportunities in Canada. Harold Mason, owner of the Mason Company in Toronto, Canada, specializing in tunnel and stone bridge construction, discovered a major gold deposit while constructing a tunnel in British Columbia. Grethe targeted Harold as a suitable suitor for Ludie, but Ludie rejected the plan, insisting that her great-grandmother Mariah's charter provided that she marry a moneyed, malleable man of her choice. Harold, a fifty-year-old divorced father of three sons, showed enthusiasm for the merger. To Ludie's dismay, Grethe ignored her rejection of Harold and placed him in charge of all mining joint ventures, including the Cíbola gold mine.

1998

Harold assigned his Canadian mine manager, Jorge Catalano, to Cíbola to implement the mining methods employed in British Columbia. Carlos IV objected to Jorge and his mistreatment of workers in the Sonora, but Grethe ignored the abusive work practices because of the high profits gained. Shortly thereafter, Carlos IV was killed in a helicopter crash, and second son, Victor, was pressed into service as Emblema Compañia President.

2000

While inspecting a job site in Kalamata, Greece, where Roadways was constructing a major, mountainous roadway, Ludie met Roland Zain, a French explosives expert from the Valais Canton in Switzerland. She assessed him to be a potential foil against Harold. Ludie and Roland lingered much too long while visiting Buck in Monte Carlo. Grethe made loud objections to Roland, proclaiming anyone of French descent to be unfit for a Carter. She berated Josiah for hiring Roland and dispatched him to Monte Carlo to fire Roland and escort Ludie back to Chapel Hill.

2001

Noah continued his restless search for a teaching career offering something of value. He finally allied himself with the Mexican Grupo Socialistas Escuelas and founded a bilingual school in the State of Chiapas in southern Mexico. He refused to agree to police – the Federales' – demands that they select his students. Tensions escalated and the school was raided by the Federales, the buildings burned, students killed, and Noah imprisoned. Josiah used his full crisis intervention skills to free Noah and return him to Chapel Hill. Josiah then announced plans to retire, so that he could reunite his family. In addition to this unwelcome news, Sarah was dismayed to discover that Noah was dating Ludie.

In the present time Grethe is killed in her massive sports utility vehicle, the all-black Intimidator, in a wreck less than twenty miles from Chapel Hill. The vehicle was hardly marked. In her will, Grethe provided that Ludie could not marry without the approval of Harold, and directed that Josiah be retired, so he couldn't employ his assertive leadership skills against Harold. The bride-capture combat for Ludie is now at full gallop. Victor insists that a more equitable business relationship between Roadways and Emblema be negotiated immediately. Harold warns that Ludie can avoid a hostile takeover by his company only by their immediate marriage. Roland urges that he join Roadways in a responsible position to intervene on her behalf in the crises confronting her.

To add to the turmoil, the Cíbola mine's ore deposit in the Mexican Sonora is depleted, and Roadways must abandon the mesa at a time when major NAFTA-related business opportunities are being negotiated. Harold orchestrates an anti-Roadways public relations campaign in the Sonora to pressure Ludie further, which draws angry, abused workers to Cíbola mesa. Victor increases the turmoils by accusing Harold of stealing gold from Emblema Compañia. Harold denies the theft and blames all of the discord on Ludie's inability to lead Roadways, offering himself as Roadways' savior. Ludie fires Harold from his Roadways' position.

On the first day of May, Sarah journeys to Oxford University to complete her doctoral program and the Carter Chronicles by month's end. Without consulting her, Ludie and Noah announce plans to marry, details to be finalized in a month. Sarah fears the role-reversal Ludie has accomplished. She is now with the mounted vanguard with her son, leaving her in the dust and the offal with a jaded Josiah. Sarah determines to accomplish two critical tasks while at Oxford. She must earn her doctoral degree and complete research on Ethel Wessex's ancestry. Sarah is near to confirming that Ethel was descended from Duke Cedric, the Wessex warrior-scholar, and, hopefully, the bold, assertive, and loyal Earl Ethelred, the Wessex warrior hero of Hastings.

Armed with scholarly achievements and warrior credentials, Sarah will depart her lifelong path as a follower, become a warrior-scholar, and demand that Ludie share Noah's loving and caring with her. Sarah was denied access to her father's loving and caring, so the complete loss of Noah to another female is unthinkable. She will risk everything to win the loving and caring that means everything to her.

# Part 1
# Cíbola Destinado

# Chapter 1

Noah Chamberlain ran north on Airport Road for ten minutes from his parents' condominium before arriving at Roadways Way. He turned left at the Carter mansion and was at the sprawling, three-story Roadways Company headquarters building in another three minutes. Noah didn't break into a sweat in the coolness of the early May Chapel Hill morning. The commute was a warm-up for his daily five-mile run.

The mind-clearing run also enabled Noah to ponder the whirlwind of events which had swept him up since his untimely departure from Chiapas, courtesy of the Federales bully boys. He was painfully aware that he was obligated to his father, Josiah, for rescuing him from the rat-infested prison by means he didn't even want to know about. Noah had worked hard to convince himself that he was no longer obligated to Josiah. Perhaps, he thought, he would learn the quid pro quo today.

His debt to Josiah was increased when his return to Chapel Hill resulted in a whirlwind romance with Ludie Carter, the new Roadways President. The windstorm became a cyclone when she proposed marriage. At first, he resisted the romance. Didn't he? Or maybe he just had doubts about the chances of a successful, long-term relationship. But he was so emotionally and physically attracted to her, he accentuated the positives and minimized the negatives. They were both now thirty-something and searching for lasting commitments. Grethe, Ludie's mother, was no longer lurking in her guard-dog mode, and Josiah would retire in a few months. Firing Harold, Ludie's failed suitor, from Roadways was a clincher for Noah, because Ludie was finally breaking away from Grethe's manipulative ways.

Their marriage would also dispel the myth that the Carter women marry only malleable men of means. As Josiah would say in what he considered to be his folksy, colorful manner, "Noah didn't have a pot to piss in or a window to throw it out." Noah had no means, so he wasn't susceptible to being shaped by Ludie. He disregarded the jealous jabs aimed at him in Chapel Hill for marrying money because of the purity of his intentions. He coveted only Ludie – his first love – and could care less about her money or position.

A couple of the ever-present protestors at ease before the security fence exchanged high-fives with Noah. NAFTA – pros and cons – seemed to be the predominating subject today. The opposing placards declared that the free trade initiative would either enrich all United States citizens at all economic levels or end fair living wages for all workers worldwide forever – no fence-sitters here. NAFTA was a hot topic for Noah in the Chiapas jungle, because it enabled him to convince Mexican workers that they must become bilingual – trilingual for the Indians of Chiapas – to enable them to work on either side of the United States border. Language skills would provide them an advantage over their English-only workplace competitors in the United States and Canada.

Before entering the building, Noah waved to Derek Warden, one-half of Ludie's wife-husband security team, noting that Derek seemed to examine him with added interest. Why not, Noah thought, the former Chamberlain kid was about to marry his boss. Patience Warden spotted Noah as soon as he entered the crowded main reception area. Noah admired her because he couldn't imagine the ex-FBI agent in need of anything from him or anyone else, the kind of person he wanted to be. Patience smiled and waved him into the elevator to the third floor executive level, designed as a decompression chamber for those entering the rarified world of top management. He paused at the elevator door to allow her to appraise fully his attire. She remembered him from earlier visits when he was a disheveled UNC student with shaggy blond beard and hair. She puzzled at the wisdom of now allowing him into the executive chambers garbed in faded blue jeans and work shirt, beard, and shaggy hair still in place. But Noah's worn blue running shoes with new red laces caused her to frown.

Josiah waited inside his large situation room, the Roadways battle-planning hub. "Glad you're here early. Ludie has moved the meeting up because all hell has broken loose at the Cíbola mesa gold mine in the Sonora. Tucson TV stations are showing old Papago Indian women flocking to Cíbola and blocking access to the mesa. Damn, we were almost out of there. Another month and our shutdown of the ore-depleted mine would've been completed."

"I thought that mine was closed years ago." Noah seated himself on a swivel chair facing Josiah, who turned from a bank of computer screens. Confronting his father at close range, he saw much of himself grown old, noting in particular the marks of age on Josiah's large hands.

"Don Carlos operated the mine at a slow but profitable level until he died, but then Grethe allowed Harold to manage all mining projects," Josiah said. "Ludie wants you to go down there and give us a hand. I can't go because a monster road construction project is up for grabs in Turkey."

Noah recognized the quid pro quo hidden within a pincer movement. "You and Ludie have decided that I'm bound for Cíbola have you? Do I have anything to say about this?"

"Hold your horses. She needs you only for a temporary assignment to help clean up the mess."

Noah shrugged. "Why me? You know I'm no good at this crisis intervention stuff you dote on. I'm not into bashing old Indian women around to save a few dollars."

"Give it a rest," Josiah said. "Roadways has a lot at stake at Cíbola. If we can get out of the Sonora without a public relations disaster, we've got the inside track on some major Mexican road construction projects."

"You must have some real assertive ball-busters around Roadways, so send one of them. How about that Roland Zain guy you champion?"

Josiah sighed. "Your assignment to Cíbola is Ludie's idea. She believes that some finesse is required, whatever-in-hell that means. Harold brought this on by the way he mistreated the Papago workers, and now Victor, Ludie's business partner in Mexico, is stirring the pot by claiming that Harold has stolen gold from him. He's also brought the Mexican Federales into the hassle. What a mess."

"So you're opposed to my assignment, a vote of no-confidence. Is that the deal?"

"As usual, you want it both ways with me, don't you? You would please Ludie and, besides, it would give you a fresh look-see at the place where we spent five very happy years, our best ever as a family. Maybe Sarah and I could join you down there when she returns from Oxford. I'm retiring soon, so we could mend some of our fences."

Josiah's ambitions were alarming news to Noah. Onrushing events in his life were threatening his highly desired maverick ways, enabling him to escape familial fences. He longed for his now-defunct humble classroom in the village of Comitan in Chiapas, where he was content on his ideal maverick path. And it wasn't his job to tell Josiah that Sarah didn't have fence-mending in mind.

Josiah surveyed Noah's beard, clothing, and colorful footwear. "Just had to do it, didn't you? I've long-since got the message that you totally disapprove of who I am and what I do, but why mock Ludie also?" After failing to convince Noah to accept his black shoes, Josiah lectured him on the difference between irreverence and ego indulgence. Noah was reminded that his maverick ways would have to end, because he would soon be a member of the Roadways leadership team.

Noah understood that Josiah's added agitation was caused by fear that his son could be his boss if he elected to do so, an alluring prospect. Apparently, Noah decided, he was indeed bound for Cíbola to please Ludie, his bride-to-be.

"Look, Noah, are you reneging?" Josiah asked. "You told Ludie you would do a few chores for Roadways this summer, so you could familiarize yourself with operations before your marriage. Now you either do it with gusto or get the hell out of here. I don't need the embarrassment."

Noah hated it when Josiah was right. "Just the thought of going in there and making business-like talk makes me cringe. She'll snicker her butt off after I've declared that I want no part of Roadways' management. I'm going to establish more bilingual schools in Mexico, and she promised to help."

"I know that things are tough for you now. It's rough to return home on a bus with a bruised body, but this is a chance to get your pride back."

Noah hated that Josiah had intervened on his behalf in Chiapas, even if it did free him from prison. "Yeah, sure, Don Josiah, I feel real proud being summoned by you to do a chore for the boss-lady." Noah noted a momentary clenching of Josiah's large fists at being called Don Josiah rather than father by his son. Noah had started this practice during his college years to show his mocking disrespect for a big-business big shot.

Josiah went to a large, flattened display of the earth on a wall marked by several dozen white and a dozen black markers. "God damn it, get a grip. Ludie's running a two-billion-dollar company in big trouble and would be better off if she didn't mess with you for this project, or for any other purpose."

Josiah examined the map and took a deep breath. "Now that Harold has been fired as manager of the mining group, I've assumed his duties. All the white and black projects are now on my platter. I told Ludie to divest the mining projects as soon as possible, but she's not listening to me. I'm only the babysitter cooped up in this room." He stabbed at a black marker south of Tucson in the Mexican Sonora. "Yeah, that's the old gold mine I started up. There are more than one hundred operational sites on this map, so the old Cíbola mesa mine is no longer any more than a speck on a gnat's ass to me if you don't care about it. But what Harold did to the Papagos down there makes me sick. They were good folks."

"I take it that you won't miss your fellow big-business big shot?"

"You bet I won't. Now I don't have to pretend to support the weasel." Josiah smiled with satisfaction.

When does Josiah start pretending to support me in what I want to do, Noah thought, and was then consoled by the thought that he would report to Ludie while at Cíbola.

Josiah attempted to rally Noah with his heavy-handed humor. "The rumor mill says you've got some free time and may be interested in making a bunch of money in a hurry. Ludie just wants you to placate the old Papago women, dispose of Roadways' assets, and vacate that mesa. Now get in there and make yourself proud."

Noah gave Josiah his rapt attention. He knew, and knew that Josiah knew, the process in action here. Noah was receiving an old fashioned, teen-age-angst pep talk. He reluctantly asked an intelligent business question. "Why did you allow Harold to acquire all those mining black markers? Grethe listened to you."

"Hell, I egged him on to do every outrageous acquisition he could find so Grethe would see what a sorry Roadways co-owner he would be. Harold's first official act would be to fire me."

"Gee, Don Josiah, show me the so-called business ethics in doing that with Roadways assets."

Josiah stared at Noah. "My business ethics at this time in my career are to protect my job so I can retire on my own terms. That smarmy bastard Harold waltzed in here and took advantage of Grethe's lack of confidence in Ludie, so I fought him the best way I knew how. You've got to learn how to win."

"Give me a reason for always winning."

"I can't give you a reason to win other than winning is the reason for competing. You've got to risk everything to win everything. You've chosen only to compete against your own expectations – nice work if you can get it."

Noah refused to engage in an all-too-familiar argument." "O.K. How do I win this charade in Ludie's office? You're the leading authority on crisis intervention."

"Don't ask. You know her better than I do." Josiah cleared his throat. "Oh, by the way, the Cíbola mine manager, Jorge Catalano, is in there with Ludie right now. She called him in to fire him, and you'll be his replacement. He may be a little testy, because he doesn't yet know the program."

* * *

The meeting in the vast corner office with a perfect view of a fish-pond in a pine grove was typical of the Carter clan. Ludie marshaled the combatants to observe the mayhem. No advanced notice, no briefing, and no prior introduction of participants permitted. She gave Noah a slight nod only.

Noah nodded to her and plunged in. "Good morning Mr. Catalano. I'm Noah Chamberlain."

Catalano, a slender, handsome man dressed in a modish brown suit, accepted Noah's handshake. "Please call me Jorge as is the practice in your country. Pardon me, but what is your function in this meeting?" He spoke English well.

"That's to be determined, Jorge," Ludie said. "Please tell me how we're going to get Roadways out of the limelight as a heartless international robber baron and labor cheater!" She perched her lanky body on the front edge of her flight-deck desk and directed Jorge and Noah to a large sofa in a corner of the spacious office.

Jorge launched his spiel. "It is a great pity Señora Grethe did not survive to witness the outstanding success of the Cíbola gold mine. Superb technology and minimum use of human resources enabled me to extract all the gold from that old mine very rapidly with only thirty percent of the work force. Those lazy, illiterate Papago Indians prevented me from doing better. Harold will attest to my professional capabilities, for I also performed superbly for him at a Canadian gold mine. It was, of course, less profitable, because Canada is over-protective of its workers."

Ludie interrupted. "Quit strutting your stuff, and tell me how I can make this embarrassment go away."

Flinching, Jorge continued his self-promotion. "Profits were huge for Roadways and Emblema. So now I have shutdown procedures well underway. All Cíbola heavy equipment has been sent to Harold's new gold mine in Nevada, and I am preparing the mining plan. All that remains to be done is to allocate the several million dollars in facilities and supplies and, of course, dispose of the priceless deep water well I constructed at the base of the mesa."

But Ludie wasn't buying. "Roadways is going to focus on quality road construction projects built by quality craftspeople, back to the basics my great-grandmother Mariah established." Ludie turned to look at a black-framed, aged photograph of a woman in her middle years that bore an unmistakable resemblance to Grethe, and would perhaps to Ludie in her later years.

Noah studied Jorge as he tugged at the knot of his necktie. The balding man was not having a good day trying to deal with Ludie, a female boss. He was certainly suffering deep culture shock. Noah decided to continue to conceal his knowledge of the Catalan culture and the Spanish language. He would need all possible advantages in the Sonora.

"I have an iron clad contract with Harold to work with no less than two other Roadways gold mines." Jorge's voice quavered with agitation "I'm sixty years old and at the height of my powers. The Nevada gold mine will be a training facility for specialist workers to operate mines in Mexico where labor rates are insignificant. Nevada will be a small mine only because its labor costs will be even higher than Canada's"

"Feel free to participate, Noah," Ludie said.

Jorge studied Noah. "So you are Josiah's son. Do I not deserve to discuss this important matter with him?"

"You're speaking to your new boss, Jorge," Ludie said. "Return to Cíbola as soon as possible and await further orders. Your future conduct will determine your Roadways future."

Noah was sorry for the uptight man as he departed the office. "How many cronies like that did Harold have?"

Ludie's dark gray suit, Noah's favorite, matched her eyes and complemented her blond hair. The high-heeled shoes she wore, as well as the short skirt, showed her fine legs to great advantage. "I'm still sorting them out. This Cíbola mess was unknown to me, thanks to Harold. Are you going down there for Josiah?"

The pincers were now squeezing Noah. "I would take on this assignment for you, Ludie, not Josiah. Maybe I've been too stiff-necked about not becoming involved in Roadways' business dealings. Buck helped out Grethe ever so often, kind of like a goodwill ambassador or something like that."

Ludie smiled, a nice event. "Please, Noah, go down there immediately, ease Jorge out, and get those libelous news clips off the Tucson TV stations. Then abandon the mesa as soon as possible without offending the Mexican government. The old Papago women can't want the mesa back. They're only after the deep well, my only valuable bargaining chip down there. This assignment is only temporary, so you will be back working on your education projects soon."

"I've got no wheels, so I'll ask Josiah to lend me the Intimidator." Noah said. "I'm sure you would like the beast out of your sight."

Shaking her head, Ludie finally acknowledged Noah's shoes. "So you're wearing those goofy shoes to show your disdain for what you call 'the business stuff.' I hoped that Josiah, the fashion policeman, would clean you up." She sighed. "You are certainly a major project, lover boy. I'll have to give you more of my undivided attention."

She closed the office door and replaced Mariah's likeness with a large photograph in a gold frame in the center of her desk. The photograph depicted Ludie and Noah at her high school junior prom, a few hours before they experienced a most amazing sexual encounter, Ludie's first. The ever-vigilant Grethe had prevented others by threatening Josiah's job. During that period, Ludie had called Grethe the Wicked Bitch of the West and did her utmost to oppose her cunning mother without direct confrontation. Apparently, Grethe had kept her crafty leadership style in place for everyone except Ludie, who was given unrelenting doses of assertiveness lifelong. Noah believed that Ludie's marriage proposal was a vestige of her failed relationship with her mother. Whatever, he thought, we have much unfinished business.

But for now, Noah had agreed, most reluctantly, to delay further couplings until their wedding night. Ludie joined Noah on the sofa and pursued her project to mold her consort-to-be more to her liking with some heavy necking. Noah adored the energy she put into this work, the reason for wearing the blue shoes with red laces. The ploy worked, because events progressed nicely, extremely nicely, on the sofa. How lucky can a guy get?

* * *

Josiah hung up the telephone when Noah entered the situation room. "Ludie says it's a go. She's buying the ten-thousand-per-month consulting fee and payment of expenses. And you can borrow the Intimidator, if you agree to report to me."

Pincer movement accomplished, thought Noah, so give up quietly. "Give me a reason."

"Harold will go nuts when you pull this off."

"Good enough," Noah said, "but I report to Ludie if you practice any of your crisis intervention crap on me."

"Whatever," Josiah said. "Please say it's a deal so I can wrap up the bids on the Turkey project."

"It's a deal. I'm Cíbola bound, or Cíbola destinado as they say in the Sonora." Noah attempted to escape the situation room before Josiah launched into his bromides for survival in the murky world of crisis intervention, to no avail.

Chalk in hand, Josiah approached a blackboard. "You're bound for Cíbola to intervene in a crisis, so you must be systematic in your approach to assure your success and survival." He wrote "what is," "what could be," and "what should be" on the board and returned to his seat, seemingly satisfied with his work. "'What is,' of course, will be the hard facts of the situation at Cíbola. Determining them is job-one and can only be done by you on site. Take nothing I've said – or anyone else – for granted."

"So I'm to be a detective? Is that my job, Don Josiah?"

"For starters, you bet. Next, develop what should be the ideal outcome to the crisis for Roadways at Cíbola. A successful crisis intervention is one that most closely approximates the ideal outcome. When you're in a hurry and have no room for error, the ideal intervention method is to be assertive, so you must use bold determination and be ready and eager for conflict. Opponents can be best dominated by getting an overview of the battle, identifying the elements crucial to your success, and controlling all critical events. I know this isn't your style, but it's important that you make an exception just for this assignment."

"You've changed the sequence." Noah was hearing the same old stuff again, so he needed to get Josiah to move on. And he certainly wasn't going to be conned into becoming an assertive bronco-buster. "Doesn't 'could be' come before the 'should be'?"

Josiah smiled, happy for a small victory. "Glad you're paying attention. 'Could be's' are all of the possible positive and negative options you identify before you pursue the 'should be'. Remember to include all seemingly limiting or impossible factors. Contingency plans are what you develop to deal with possible negative outcomes that would prevent you from accomplishing the 'should be'."

"I've no need for your belt-and-suspenders approach. Contingency planning is the hobgoblin of the control freak. I'm remaining a maverick so I can ignore leadership doctrine and operate on my own terms. Kind of a Pancho Villa approach."

"It's way past time for you to outgrow being a maverick heretic. It's the hallmark of a self-centered, self-serving person who seeks personal freedom without responsibilities." Josiah got up and cleared the blackboard. "I hoped that your escapade in the Chiapas had taught you a lesson. As a self-declared idealist, don't you tend to see things as they should be?"

"The lesson learned in Chiapas is that there seems to be no way to escape your unwanted surveillance in the name of protecting me. Give it up, Don Josiah, and mind your own business."

Noah caught the keys to the Intimidator tossed at him, shrugged, and left the situation room. Before he left the building, he visited the engineering department on the second floor to gather some useful information about Cíbola. This isn't contingency planning, Noah assured himself, but just a little fact gathering to shorten his stay at Cíbola. After departing from the building, he realized that his verbal thrusts at Josiah were an effort to fend off a reconciliation that would bring him back to the Chamberlain household, a path he had long since rejected.

During Noah's return run to his parents' condominium, he made special note of Chapel Hill's pleasant, peaceful mid-morning ambience, knowing that he was soon to return to Mexico where people were struggling to survive. He understood that he was using the upbeat, affluent community's environment to bolster his resolve to live in villages that were the mirror opposite. Noah's unique upbringing had made this his career path of choice, but that didn't mean that it was an easy course for him to endure.

He had long puzzled over how he could marry and ask his wife and children to accept his meager lifestyle. Marrying Ludie solved this dilemma in a way he had never dared to hope for. She was the love of his life, but he had long since considered her to be unobtainable. Evidently, she did understand what he was all about. While others were tackling crises of significance in major organizations, he was attempting to intervene in a small way in the lives of poor people born in a climate of crises with no opportunity to escape unless educated.

While stuffing his few belongings into a duffel bag, Noah thought of calling Sarah and complaining that he was now reporting directly to Josiah on a Roadways' crisis intervention assignment. A ruckus and rescue would follow. Then Noah reminded himself that Saran was angry at him for the first time ever for becoming engaged to Ludie. He would go to Cíbola, do the chores assigned him, and hustle back to Ludie. By then, maybe Ludie would agree to include Sarah in their plans. Then, armed with Ludie's loving and caring, and a modicum of financial support, he would return to his own maverick path. Thus far, the course had been filled with potholes and detours, but it was all his.

# Chapter 2

Noah let Intimidator have its head as they rumbled along major highways from North Carolina to the upper Mexican Sonora, halting only for brief rests. The big, black modified war machine charged along at a steady sixty-five miles per hour. Other automobiles didn't draw near, thanks to its three ton, seven-foot-wide bulk and sixteen-inch ground clearance. Noah was soon a guilty fan of this Roadways one hundred thousand dollar asset, a latter-day macho manifestation of a war horse.

According to Noah's calculations, Jorge was now only about thirty-six hours ahead of him. Border guards at Nogales waved Noah through the inspection process. He approached Cíbola in the bright sunlight of Sunday mid-morning. The vehicle's global position finder confirmed that he was one hundred miles south of Nogales, heading east from the village of Imuris. The high isolated mesa of his boyhood that would be visible beyond the next elevation was in the vanguard of the Sierra Madre Occidental Range. Noah noted the Papago shrine-site village a mile north of the mesa's northern cliffs.

Intimidator was parked several yards off the narrow paved roadway, facing east and the mesa. Noah opened the dark-tinted windows, so he could enjoy the smell of high desert air. But, although the winds were westerly, the stench of industrial wastes struck him. At that moment, a caravan of three military vehicles appeared over the rise to the east. The middle vehicle stopped opposite Intimidator, as if to commune with a like kind. The insignia of the Mexican Federales marked all three vehicles. Two dark-tinted side windows were lowered several inches. A voice emitted from the rear window, and a gun barrel from the fore.

The demanding voice was baritone, the language Spanish. "How are you called?"

Noah's Spanish language skills were excellent, but he made his words in Spanish halting. He had dealt with the Federales in Chiapas, vowing never again to give them an opportunity to batter his body and burn his school and all his possessions.

"My name is Noah Chamberlain."

"You are alone?"

"I am."

"You are armed?

Noah hated guns. "No firearms."

A neutral tone entered the voice. "Please approach and present your credentials."

A manicured hand from the rear window accepted and soon returned Noah's passport. "Pass on by, Noah Chamberlain. Congratulations on your new assignment, and, of course, your engagement to Ludie. You have surely won two great prizes."

Sardonic laughter from the front window and breakneck Spanish assured all that here was yet another Anglo pendejo, a scurvy, sorry fool.

"May I know your name?" Noah asked.

"Why not? I am called Victor Emblema, President of Emblema Compañia."

The caravan moved on and Noah broke his phone silence with Chapel Hill, enabling him to learn from an anxious Josiah that Victor had occupied Cíbola mesa yesterday. According to Harold's gold guards still on duty, Jorge left the mesa before his arrival and had not returned. It appeared that Victor was intent on pressing his claim that Harold stole gold from Emblema Compañia, Noah was to watch his butt and check in with Captain Apache Guardia at the security gate at the top of the mesa. Noah cut the connection when Josiah second-guessed himself and ordered him to return to North Carolina.

Childhood memories of Cíbola mesa for Noah were of a new, white-washed adobe home on the brow of a high mesa that afforded a view of the vast, pristine desert. To his horror, the western side of the lone mesa was a blighted slope of stinking effluent, a cluster of structures perched on its western rim. A winding entry road was built over the waste materials dumped from inside the mesa. From the west, it didn't look to be fifteen hundred feet above the desert floor nor to occupy six square miles. Halfway up the twisting road, Noah encountered clusters of old Indian women hunkered by the roadside before piles of rocks and little fires. All turned away in a contemptuous manner save for an old woman near the mesa's rim in a worn campesino hat, who stared at him with intense interest.

Noah drove to the metal gates cemented into a high rock wall that sealed the mesa rim. The gates were opened by a sergeant to reveal a lone man slouching in the center of the roadway, finger tips of his right hand touching the back of one of two plastic folding chairs positioned at a rickety card table. Nine troopers stood at attention a few paces behind him.

A nod of the lone man's head brought the sergeant to face Noah in Intimidator. "Por favor, Señor, Captain Guardia wishes you to present your credentials. Your vehicle must be searched."

Guardia was dressed as a rodeo rider. The cant of his black hat, Captain insignias on squared shoulder, and a large pistol in his belt all marked him as a dominating force. He removed his hat to avoid Noah's offer of a handshake. Guardia's brutal, pitted face was level with

Noah's face. He was of a slender build but had large hands and feet.

Guardia's guttural voice eliminated the lilt from the Spanish he spoke. "My name's Guardia, and my job's Captain in the Federales. You can't be the new Anglo director, because you lack the fine clothes and an arrogant aspect."

Incredible, Noah thought, there's no place to hide from the Federales, even here on this destroyed mesa. "But I'm Jorge's replacement." He again spoke in halting Spanish. "Tell me of his whereabouts, Guardia."

"Your Spanish is poor and a little effeminate." Guardia said.

"And yours is very bucolic." Noah turned at a clatter behind him to observe six soldiers searching Intimidator. "Wasn't my vehicle searched at the border?"

"No, your ass was kissed in Nogales. You have the look of a mafioso drug runner or perhaps a pimp with those splendid blue shoes with red laces. Don't try to return across that border checkpoint without much bribe money in your hand."

"Again, Guardia, tell me how may I find Jorge."

Guardia seated himself and waited for Noah to do so. "Jorge's presence is of no concern to you at this moment. You're to deal with me. Your Anglo arrogance or director status can't alter this fact. I'm the law in the Sonora, and you are but an Anglo seeker of gold. You have temporary command of Cíbola mesa, no more. Don't under any circumstances involve yourself in any outside matters. You're Señor Inside and I'm Señor Outside. We agree on this, no?"

"We have no such agreement."

A soldier brought Guardia Noah's passport and returned to the reformed rank of nine.

Guardia presented Noah his passport with a slight nod. "Bueno, this is but a little test for the new boy in town. Your cojónes are being weighed, for you must have big balls to remain in the Sonora." Even while saying these conciliatory words, Guardia replaced his hat at an aggressive angle and folded his arms across his chest, a charade for his troops and the few people peering from nearby shacks.

Noah began to sweat in the increasing mid-morning heat. He was playing a part in a tableau of Guardia's design. He recalled the videos provided Tucson TV stations branding Roadways as a thief of Mexican gold occupying a destroyed mesa stolen from the Papago Indians. Josiah said that Sonora news hounds were providing videos at a profit to themselves and great embarrassment to Roadways.

"Are we to be in a news video?" Noah asked.

"Why ask? Do you have starring ambitions in the Sonora?"

Suddenly, eight soldiers hustled four manacled men past Noah into a military vehicle parked by the inside of the wall.

"Estupendo," Guardia said. "Harold's Canadian gold wagon guards have been apprehended, surely in record time. The theft of Emblema gold has been solved. Please communicate this excellent police work to your superiors." He stood and hooked thumbs in his gun belt. "You have a tranquil day."

"Hold on now!" Noah stood, knocking his chair to the ground. "Why have you arrested those men? They were inside the mesa."

"I remember our division of duties, Señor Inside. But I give you a one-time, brief instruction in my true craft as a detective. These men had the opportunity to steal gold bullion as they escorted it to Hermosillo. They clearly possessed the means and were highly moti-vated by Anglo greed. They offer no alibis, even false ones. Thanks to me, you will be able to focus on Roadways' retreat and soon rid the Sonora of all Anglo conquistadors. Proceed with haste."

Guardia held a brief conference with the sergeant and pointed up-slope. "Sergeant Chiricahua tells me that Emilio, the specialist powder man, awaits outside the maintenance building to guide the new direc-tor about the mesa."

Noah kicked his chair on the ground. "What's the name of your superior, Guardia? Are the gold wagon guards being whisked off to Hermosillo to conceal Harold's theft, Victor's theft, or your own?"

Guardia's large hands gave Noah mocking applause. "A bravura performance. Your Spanish has improved remarkably. Sergeant Chiricahua will take command of gate security and will remain until I replace him, but you're advised to improve your manners."

"Why waste my time." Noah booted the chair again. "Good manners are needed only if you encounter good-mannered folks to use them on. This is a typical Federales set-up. I was told only that Victor accused Harold of gold theft, no more. Now, just as I appear on the scene, you've orchestrated a charade to convince me to accept the guilt of four Anglos. I'm not buying this bullshit."

"This little contest is certainly a checkmate against you." Guardia eyed Noah's downed chair. "Welcome to the Sonora, Señor Inside."

Noah drove Intimidator from the gatehouse, passing through a divided ghost town. Gone were the surging spring and lush vegetation of his childhood memories. To the south were several acres of silent gold ore processing facilities. An equal area of houses occupied the north side of the road – some adobe but mostly tin shacks. None appeared to be occupied, nor did the few shops that faced the road. He had no clue as to the whereabouts of the house he occupied with his parents and his brother. A huge, sheet metal maintenance building and a new, trim guesthouse were on the eastern outskirts of the housing area.

The Indian man lazing on the bench before the maintenance building approached Noah the moment he got out of Intimidator. He was a handsome man, not young or old, and he spoke Spanish. "Hola, are you at last the new pajaro gordo, the Roadways big-wig?" The man examined Noah's clothes, shaggy hair and beard, and Intimidator still creaking and snapping from the long journey from North Carolina. "Of course not, when does he arrive?"

Noah managed a tired smile. "Sorry to disappoint you, but I'm the new big-wig, a real big-shot as you can see. How are you called?"

The man suddenly straightened and smiled expansively. "I'm Emilio, a powder man specialist, who lives with my new wife, Rosa, in the guest house. Rosa is Señor Catalano's cook and housekeeper. Are we to be dispossessed?"

"Por favor, show me what you must, and we'll discuss your future employment tomorrow. Should we walk or ride?"

Emilio's eyes gleamed as he reappraised Intimidator. "We must ride by all means."

When Noah drove to the inner rim of the mesa, his stomach did a flip-flop. A mining pit at least two miles across opened before them, the bottom surely as deep as the mesa's height. Noah envisioned a halved boiled egg with its golden center removed, but the walls were scarred and jumbled from the fevered hunt for treasure. A wide, clockwise-spiral road from point of entry to the pit's bottom imposed a heavy-handed discipline on the pit. Harold's broad road to conquer this Cíbola Empire with giant machines ran roughshod over all natural features, save one.

Emilio pointed ahead as Intimidator started their descent. "The Great Corúa is a place of great importance that I must show the new managing director before we journey to the bottom of the pit and return to view the mesa top. Please halt now."

Noah climbed up a sloping slab of concrete surrounding a massive basalt pillar that jutted from the pit wall to a height exceeding fifty feet. The so-called Great Corúa was certainly an anomaly, Noah thought. It was a hell of a phallic symbol that caused a swerve in the otherwise symmetrical spiral of the road to the bottom of the pit. The base was encased in concrete as part of an effort to ensure the safety of the road. Four cables girdled the Corúa one-third up from its base, anchoring it to the pit wall uphill by four massive metal fittings at ten-foot intervals.

Noah recognized rampant engineering overkill at work.

The decided outward cant of the pillar provided a sheltered place at the downhill base. Emilio beckoned Noah to join him at this suggestion of a grotto. "You may make offerings if you wish. The Great Corúa serves all, perhaps even Anglos."

Noah pointed to a large metal door in the pit wall below the Great Corúa.

Emilio anticipated a question. "That's a powder bunker now holding many old, unstable explosives. Other bunkers were built as we deepened the pit. Do you wish admittance to this dangerous place?"

"No, it's best we delay our tour until tomorrow because I need sleep."

Emilio nodded. "I'll show you to the room in the guest house once reserved for Señor Mason." His ever-present smile was apologetic. "So sorry, Señor, but then I must go to the lower service plaza and continue to move all explosives to this main storage bunker. Rosa will have your mid-day meal ready in the hospitality suite when you wish."

Noah almost told Emilio that he would forage for himself, but Emilio's pleading look stopped him.

"Por favor, Rosa is afraid she is fired if you don't use her services." Emilio said. "She has been Señor Catalano's housekeeper for the past few years and fears the worst. I've work because I'm one of the workers with great skills who arrived at Cíbola with Señor Catalano. I'm the jefe, the boss, of all powder men. Specialists were housed in the homes of dispossessed Papago unskilled workers, who were forced to join the labor gang applying each day for jobs. It was a pity, but I needed work."

"Has Jorge returned?" Noah was getting the picture.

"No, Señor."

"You've had your lunch?"

"S?, Señor."

"Then I'll see you later."

After returning to the mesa rim, Noah walked to the guesthouse and entered the open door of a room devoted to the preparation and consumption of food and drink. Roadways stockholders certainly provided Harold and Jorge with many creature comforts. A small, comely Indian woman was placing a platter on a serving bar.

"Hola, Rosa, I'm Noah Chamberlain."

Rosa examined Noah with surprise. "Por favor, Señor, be seated where I've placed your coffee."

"Will you join me for lunch?"

"No, gracias, I took my food with Emilio." Rosa's smile was wary.

Noah remained standing. "Perhaps you'll take another coffee with me. I must speak to you of Jorge."

Rosa stood fast. "I'm not comfortable being at the table with the patrón, the big boss."

"Are you comfortable speaking to me here?" Noah stood by the serving bar.

"Am I fired if I don't speak of Señor Catalano?"

"Yes, of course, so is Emilio, perhaps others." Noah furrowed his brow to help conceal his lie.

Rosa wasn't a fountain of information. She admitted that Jorge had a big home and an old wife in Barcelona and that the marriage was not a happy one. She shed some of her wariness. "The wife will not accompany him on his journeys. He hated to come to this place but had no choice. He needed money for his life, and he needed to work, always his work."

"So where was Jorge Saturday and today, Rosa?" Noah asked. "Does he desert his duties often?"

"No, no, Senor Catalano is most punctual and does very hard work." Rosa looked away from Noah. "Perhaps he went to the old Papago shrine place north of the mesa now called Libertad. It's now a place of debauchery, truly a sinful place. But Emilio no longer goes there since we declared our marriage last month."

Noah took four corn cakes from the table as he departed. "Gracias, Rosa."

"But, Señor, do you take your meals here? Am I to clean your room?"

"I'll gladly take my meals here. The room will be cleaned by myself."

*  *  *

Noah was awakened in the guesthouse room by the return of an old nightmare tormentor and knew it to be five o'clock in the morning without looking at his wristwatch. He wasn't surprised that the Chiapas village of Comítan's school grounds killing of five students, his Kent State, was again taunting him in his dreams. His usual prescription was to arise and do his five-mile run. This morning he dressed to report for work.

Resisting the urge to explore in the cool morning air, Noah hurried to the maintenance building to call Josiah and give him a so-far, so-good, so-what report. He entered a lighted office and found it to be occupied.

"Please enter, Noah." Jorge was seated at a desk smoking a slender cigar in a gold holder. He looked to be hugely hung over, his eyes woeful and dark-rimmed. His desk was orderly. A framed metallurgical engineering diploma from the University of Barcelona occupied one corner next to a well-used assay scales in a finely-crafted teak box. A photograph of an aristocratic old man was the only other item visible. A worktable behind the desk held a large computer. Wall decorations were fine water colorings of Ramblas Avenida street scenes in Barcelona and a Gaudiesque mansion atop a craggy promontory overlooking the ancient city and seaport.

Noah shook Jorge's proffered hand and bowed slightly to the older man. "Sorry to barge in, but I need to call Chapel Hill. Do you prefer to speak Spanish?"

"Spanish is never preferred, because I am Catalan. I understand your Spanish is excellent after all." He paused. "I am sorry that I disrespected you in Chapel Hill. I did not know that you are Ludie's intended husband."

"No, no, it's I who disrespected you by my silence. I'm not really a Roadways employee. This temporary assignment is only a favor for Ludie. But now I must inform Josiah of the situation at Cíbola regarding the gold wagon guards."

"I understand that the guards have been taken to Hermosillo at the vagaries of the Mexican police state, which are no better than Spain's. I do not know what happened, because I was inspecting the deep water well north of the mesa Saturday."

"Can Victor assist me?"

Jorge shrugged. "No, for he whistles the tune, and Guardia does the dance. History is strange indeed. Are not Spaniards and Apaches strange fellows to be in the same bed?" He looked at the photograph of the old man. "I represent a thousand years of Catalanos, even in my lowly state on this mesa. The name of this mesa, Cíbola, also does honor to my father, Juame Catalano, the last to control the Banco de Cataluna. When I was a boy, he told me of the stories of great riches and a perfected life possible in the Americas in the Seven Cities of Cíbola, a golden heaven on earth. And Juame believed that the Catalanos would prevail and win, always. But he died, and I was dispossessed from Catalonia and the Catalano ancestral mansion by a cunning wife who evicted me without any direct conflict whatsoever. She accomplished in a few months what the Moors were unable to do over eight hundred years. Before I die, I am sworn to accumulate the funds to repossess my home."

He took the photograph in his hand. "Victor's accusations of gold theft are a continuation of the feud between the Catalanos and the Emblemas. Victor's lowbrow family claim that my ancestors confiscated their share of gold from the Americas three centuries ago. Emblemas have possessed the Banco de Cataluna since Franco's war, but they paid with much pale Spanish blood. All have long memories in Iberia."

"I can't afford to get involved in local politics again," Noah said. "I'm here to shutdown Cíbola as soon as possible while trying to placate the Papagos."

Jorge placed his cigar holder in a gold case. "If a minor matter is addressed, I would welcome the opportunity to help you execute your shutdown project."

"What minuscule problem troubles Carlomagnos' descendent?" Noah asked, knowing that Charlemagne the Great loomed large in Catalan history since the eighth century.

"I need a suitable position." Jorge smiled with appreciation. "I am past my sixtieth year and, given the ways of mining enterprises, have never accumulated pension security. I would be the perfect managing director of the Nevada gold mine training facility. Harold made such a promise to me. Would you intercede with Ludie on my behalf?"

"I'll speak to her." Noah recognized a barter advantageous to him. "How may I assist you?"

"Let's review the shutdown progress and problems before I call Josiah."

Emilio, with a smile, brought in coffee, hot corn cakes, and honey. He was not subservient, making ready eye contact as he attended them. Noah, a life-long member of the eat-lots-but-stay-trim club, wolfed three corn cakes down while Jorge removed materials from his desk drawer. According to Josiah, he was a premier gold mine manager with a long record of successful performances at mine sites on four continents.

"Our shutdown does not go well," Jorge said. "The last of the gold bars from our refinery were escorted to Hermosillo by the gold wagon guards one month ago. All mobile equipment has been transferred to the gold ore deposit in Nevada, but all other equipment, supplies, and facilities are yet to be inventoried, allocated to Emblema or Roadways, or sold. Ludie and Victor are contending for ownership of the well and its water. This extraordinary well will be a powerful bargaining device with the Mexican government." He placed a binder before Noah. "These materials include the closing financial statements that certify how I extracted one hundred million American dollars worth of gold. Cíbola's mining and milling costs of only one hundred and twenty dollars per ounce is now a new industry low."

Noah nodded his encouragement and eyed a corn cake that must be considered to be Jorge's.

Jorge pushed the platter to Noah. "Harold always expressed great satisfaction with my efforts. But Victor carped about his discontent from day one of our operations, because I am a Catalano."

"Does Victor have cause?" Noah asked.

"It is not possible. Harold assured me that Victor received his promised share. My superior, mechanized mining and milling methods produced more than the measure of gold Victor was promised. And my methods improved efficiencies, cut labor costs, and unduly confused Victor with higher than anticipated profits. He is but a vapid playboy licking his chops for increased wealth for little effort."

"What's blocking the completion of the shutdown project?"

"The old Papago women calling themselves the dispossessed. They have gathered along the roadway to Cíbola in increasing numbers since operations were discontinued. I did not permit unskilled Papagos to occupy houses on the mesa, relying on specialists imported and daily labor applicants at a rallying point three miles from our gate. Each shift was bussed to and from the rally arena. The old women often impede operations by moving to the road center. Now we have only Tomas Mechanico and his family and Emilio and Rosa in residence, aside from myself. And, now, Sergeant Chiricahua and Trooper Perez guarding the gate."

"Do you go to Libertad?"

"Yes, but of course. My wife of convention only for many years lives in Barcelona. Some of the girls are most obliging when you have sexual needs. It is most convenient." Jorge massaged his temples. "But I lingered too long Saturday at the drinking place and hurled my stomach. I was unable to rise from the bed Sunday – most unusual, for I am a temperate man."

"Tell me more of the Papago workers." Noah said, not dismayed by Jorge's cavalier attitude, his assertive crisis intervention credentials now all-too-well established.

"Except for specialists, other workers are interchangeable human resources in my methods," Jorge said. "I insisted that the Papago workers live off mesa and not consume time, space, or resources."

"So most specialists have been reassigned?"

"Or more likely terminated or placed on leave without pay." This waste saddened Jorge. "The Nevada gold mine operation decisions are important to the future employment of many, including myself. The need for job security makes cowards of all of us."

"Who could steal gold from this mesa?"

"As I confided to you, I know nothing of police matters, and I wish to remain ignorant. My concentration is the mining and refining of precious metals. Most poor workers would gladly steal. And, of course, many jobs were lost because of my work methods."

Noah shifted his position to eyeball to eyeball. "Jorge, you're doing a tap dance. Is it because I'm an Anglo, or are you only mildly interested in employment in Nevada? I've got to know."

"I know not your training, but long experience has made me very callous. This maintenance building and the guest house are on the very ground where the infirmary and school house stood when the mine was first constructed, and, of course, the site of the water source called the Birth Spring. It is necessary to destroy the monuments each culture builds on high ground."

"To break their spirits?"

"No, no, Noah, only to encourage them to abandon the site without bloodshed."

"Ah, a spirited, orderly departure was engineered, is that it?"

"Please, Noah, do not ask me to defend this tactic. I was told by Harold that this was not my concern, because I was only an engineer of mining and refining." The litany continued. "And I needed a job."

"Jorge, you've switched from a tap dance to a zarzuela. Favor me with your best guess of how a gold theft could possibly occur."

"Perhaps Victor Emblema hired men to steal the gold once it left the mesa. Sometimes Spaniards do these things for sport. Please, Noah, no more, for this is only dangerous conjecture."

"One last question, what's the score on the gold wagon guards? Could they be guilty as charged?"

Jorge finally spoke from gut feelings. "As is the uniform practice in gold extracting operations, the gold wagon guards were hired by Harold from an outside agency. They safeguard the gold bars from the moment they leave the melting and molding unit to deposit at a refinery. We had such guards for delivering our large gold bars to Hermosillo. They dispatched these duties in an exemplary manner, meeting each and every audit requirement. My spotless record for integrity is intact. Please do not soil it. This I cannot tolerate."

"Sorry, I surely wasn't questioning your professional effectiveness in extracting and safeguarding the gold," Noah said.

"It is I who am sorry." Jorge took a deep breath. " Harold selected me from many candidates for his British Columbia mine and was as quick to praise as to criticize. I kept four of the guards for security of the mesa after shutdown was announced. They were good at gold wagon guarding and bad at people control. But how do we replace them? Captain Guardia's soldiers are good at control and intimidation, but not loyal to us."

"I'll work on that, and you continue with the shutdown schedule you've developed."

"And you will concern yourself with convincing all that no gold theft occurred?"

"Sure, I'll work on it." Noah's favored scenario was that no gold was stolen, so he could leave the contentious citizens of the Sonora to fight their own battles.

Jorge started to light a cigar, noted Noah's gaze of disapproval, and put it aside. "It was reported to me by Chiricahua last evening when I returned to Cíbola that Guardia has quarantined you to the mesa. A pity because there are many places of great interest in this area. Some say another Cíbola-like gold deposit exists to the east. I believe this to be true"

He cleared his desk of papers, leaving the binder for Noah. "Bottom line, as Norte Americanos say, is that the old Papago women are holding hostage several million dollars worth of assets on the mesa. Victor welcomes this chaos and is bedeviling Harold and Roadways through the Tucson TV with false claims of gold thefts to induce Roadways to restructure their Mexican joint venture agreements. He wants more money for doing less, a true playboy this Spaniard. I will vacate this office for now so that you may call Josiah. Emilio will prepare another for you shortly."

Before calling Josiah, Noah fell into his old routine of scripting his conversation to avoid direct confrontations. By the time he was in high school, Noah had learned that Josiah didn't tend to differentiate between large and small crises in Noah's life. He would return home from far-flung, big business battlegrounds intent on doing his fatherly chores as soon as possible by wiping out all of Noah's problems. Josiah would frequently use a howitzer when a pellet gun was appropriate, so Noah crafted his communications carefully to induce Josiah to hold his fire.

# Chapter 3

Upon calling Roadways headquarters in Chapel Hill, Noah got shot in the foot by falling for Josiah's easy opening gambit. Josiah listened with patience as Noah related yesterday's incidents, making the locals almost comic-operatic. Josiah gave supportive "un-huhs" as Noah capsulated Jorge's report. He showed particular interest in Noah's assertion that a newly-appointed Federales Captain, named Guardia, was throwing his weight around to impress Victor, probably Guardia's sponsor for his own recent job promotion.

Josiah snapped the hammer. "Noah, you were seen on TV this morning being bullied by a Federales captain on our property. The word is that he has solved the gold theft to Victor's liking by jailing the gold wagon guards." He paused for breath. "Ludie just chewed on me big time for not being on top of this fiasco. Victor or Harold has just hosed you. Do you understand?"

Noah allowed that he did. Josiah pressed him for details such as the means for the supposed gold theft, how and when it was accomplished, the names of suspects other than the guards, and the alibi offered by the men arrested. Noah admitted vast ignorance, protesting that he was hired to shut down Cíbola, not assist the stupid Federales. Josiah shouted that Noah's assignment was now confined to solving the gold thefts, because Victor had frozen all remaining Cíbola assets in Mexico. The "what is" he was to determine was the truth of the gold theft accusations.

The telephone recorded the whap of Josiah's office door closing, a certain clue that he was steamed. He ticked off the tasks that Noah was to complete, speaking like a man with forty years of rough-and tumble construction experience. His resume included assignments as on-site czar of many contentious projects in terrorist playpens. Remember K.I.S.S., Josiah said. Keep It Simple, Stupid. Make no assumptions about anything and trust only reliable, verifiable information.

Josiah asked if he understood, and Noah said he did. Let's hope so, Josiah said, because Noah had to get to the bottom of the gold theft accusations. Go out and collect some alibis and even a few clues, Josiah insisted, noting that a smart-ass like Noah could sort through them in record time. Noah hated irony when it was heaped on him. He never mentioned this to Josiah, who peppered him with added instructions and ended the tirade by warning Noah to forget bailing out on his temporary assignment. Noah realized that he was in a nightmare rivaling Chiapas – working for Josiah in a crisis begging for assertive behavior. And he hated it when Josiah used his ball-buster business voice, now directed at him and doubling the aggravation.

"O.K., Don Josiah, I get the message. You're paying me the big bucks to handle any crap tossed on me, no job too dirty or dangerous. But I need help because Guardia assures me that I'm less than nothing outside Cíbola. I'll hold this fort down if you will authorize some outside help to sort out the financial disputes between Ludie, Harold, and Victor. You know I'm not interested in that kind of stuff."

"Then what in hell is Ludie up to sending you down there?" Josiah snorted and then sighed. "Dammit, you're not qualified for this combat, so you by all means stay on that mesa with the security gate locked. Guardia's doing you a favor. The debacle of the old Papago women now blocking the gate to Cíbola is being shown on TV stations in Arizona and New Mexico. Worse yet, CNN made a reference on their national news. I'm giving you hell, because you can't fail this Cíbola assignment. The Chamberlains' reputation is on the line, and I'm not leaving this company a loser. Let Jorge handle the shutdown chores for now."

He lost his snarl. "I've actually had Wayne Coffer working on this Cíbola financial flap for the last month. He retired last year from Roadways and will be calling you soon."

"What are his qualifications?"

"Suffice it to say that he's the guy that I would want in my foxhole. He was Roadways internal audits director because he won't take a con or crap from anyone. Now, hang up, go to work, and watch your back."

* * *

Noah bolted from the maintenance building as soon as he completed his conversation with Josiah. He prowled among the adobe houses and tin shacks but failed to identify his boyhood home. A seat on a bench on the rickety porch of a vacant general store afforded Noah a view of the operations half of the property across the roadway to the south. It was clean and orderly in comparison to the residential side. No scrap or waste materials insulted this area, but they were dumped haphazardly in abundance among the residences.

The ever-present feelings of self-disgust for being born an Anglo-Saxon gripped Noah amidst the proof-positive of the total disregard for the possessions loved and cared for by cultures foreign to them. And the callous destruction of the natural beauty and lifestyles on the mesa was very personal and hurtful to him. This once-bewitching place had represented Noah's ideal of what life should be. At age nine, he secretly declared himself to be a Papago Indian in spirit, and in contempt of his skin, hair, and eye colors. In the intervening years, he discovered no reasons to change his mindset.

A Papago woman, Maru, who was supposed to be Sarah's domestic servant but became her sister-like confidant. They were the instruments of his early conversion. Sarah was an ideal mother. She was wise beyond her years and possessed boundless patience to listen and respond to the needs, wants, and endless questions of Josh and Noah and Maru's daughter, Habita, who was Noah's age. Maru was a fantastic teller of Papago folk tales that had come to represent for Noah a far more sensible version of the spiritual world than the sporadic attempts at Christian indoctrination received from infrequent visits by itinerant circuit riders.

Oidak, Maru's husband and Habita's father, was a Papago manifestation of Puck, a truly gifted, trickster sprite. He could perform such miraculous feats as wiggling his ears without visible effort, make pebbles disappear from his fist and reappear anywhere, and project his voice into hand puppets of his own making. Oidak could perform many more wonders, and had done so while not under the close supervision of Maru. He could hurl a stone farther than any man in the tribe and defeat all comers at arm wrestling, even Josiah, to the delight of all.

In those past golden days, Josiah had gladly served as Oidak's dupe for his shenanigans, never fearing for the erosion of his patrón status. And for good reason for it had cemented the Papago people's high regard for Don Josiah, the big man with a large, fun-loving heart and no Anglo pretensions. Sarah observed the frolics in her wistful way, content because her sons were receiving ample loving and caring. As the years passed, Noah came to understand that Oidak's pranks actually served to integrate and reconcile the Anglo and Papago cultures existing on the mesa.

While Noah mourned his departure from Cíbola, Sarah gladly traveled on to other duty stations, ever eager to discover what the next twist or turn in their path might reveal. She had urged Josiah to continue his battles to climb the Roadways Company career path ladder, as if his elevated status might have revealed a more meaningful path for her.

As an adult, Noah negated the love he had for Josiah while at Cíbola, where his life was idyllic within his extended loving, caring family on the secure high mesa. After experiencing the ugly realities existing elsewhere, he had become increasingly angry and resentful of Josiah for depriving him of this sanctuary only to pursue his own selfish path to becoming big-business big shot. And he had witnessed the changes for the worse – in his estimation – in Josiah's behavior. He had become increasingly assertive at work and at home. The loving and caring parent-patrón who could be a clown disappeared.

Noah returned to the realities of his present situation on Cíbola. Having stealthily studied the mine and mill material flow charts while in Chapel Hill, he could now visualize this model of technological effectiveness from drilling, blasting, and hauling from the pit to crushing, milling, leaching, and melting in the facilities he was viewing. Ore was melted into one-hundred-and-fifty-pound bars of impure gold and sold to refiners who processed them into high purity gold bullion. These marvels of processing excellence were to be dismantled and shipped to locations to be determined. This included the two large water towers above the ore processing area, each capable of supplying several Mexican villages. A pipeline from north of the mesa, at least two feet in diameter, connected to the tanks.

Jorge sounded the horn of a high-riding, blue truck and waved at Noah as he drove to the operations area. The vehicle had a "Cíbola" sign lettered in gold on its door.

"More, Señor?" Emilio materialized and offered, with a smile, a pot of coffee, a cup, and a covered plate on a tray.

"Muchas gracias." Noah made room on the bench for the tray and watched Emilio depart. The plate held fried eggs on toast and a generous portion of refried beans. As he ate, he reflected on the sad plight of the people who had once inhabited the mesa, before modern-day conquistadors arrived. No Sonora people prospered, only greedy overlords. And now the people were dispossessed from their homes, as well as their jobs.

Blatant thievery of irreplaceable natural resources by greedy outside invaders, Noah thought. He now saw the awful hierarchy from his recent repositioning at the top of the survival pile, Ludie's groom-to-be. But from the bottom, basic needs were water for today, then food, and then shelter from the harsh elements. Jobs that could assure water, food, and shelter for tomorrow could then be considered. Toss in sex and religion, and other means of self-actualization, Noah thought, and that provides the only schematic needed to understand how the dispossessed existed. Greed, that selfish desire beyond reason, how does it fit into this simplistic framework? Noah recalled Maru's boyhood story of sharing practiced by the Papagos. Anything owned in excess of immediate needs was portioned out to clan members. He reflected that his Anglo-Saxon ancestors were absent the day that natural law was passed.

The ever-present, smiling Emilio materialized and escorted Noah to a workmanlike, large office in the maintenance building, informing Noah that the office was once Harold's. The walls were covered with detailed engineering drawings of the mine and ore extraction facilities.

"Coffee, Señor Chamberlain?" Emilio placed a cup of coffee on his desk.

"Gracias, Emilio, would you please call me Noah.

Emilio's smile was uncertain." Truly, I'm to call you by your given name? You are the patrón."

"A temporary job only. I would be honored if you would do so." Noah pointed at the stacks of file cases visible from an inner office window." You and Jorge are making progress with the inventory, sí?"

"Sí, Señor Noah, progress is being made. Señor Jorge makes it so. He's a very efficient man. Each file case has a different destination in the warehouse on the other side of the road. I know all except the four cases to the left. Habita Mechanico, the school teacher who also is a filing clerk, hasn't advised me."

"Habita means little bean. Are many Papago women called this name?"

"I know of only one Habita. She has always lived on this mesa according to Rosa."

"Could you direct me to her?" Noah asked." I once knew a Habita."

Emilio beckoned Noah to accompany him, walking at a brisk pace and saying nothing. He stopped before a nondescript adobe dwelling with an open front door.

"Enter, por favor," Emilio said." I'll bring Habita from the little garden she attempts to grow nearby."

Noah entered and was amazed to see that the interior was beautifully decorated and furnished. He moved to the open doorway of a second room that would offer a view of the desert far below. Noah froze, eyes riveted on an interior wall. A large watercolor likeness of Oidak was on the wall, placed there by Sarah when he was seven years old. Memories flooded him. This was his bedroom for five years. The sudden clarity of these recollections made him stagger against the door frame.

Emilio spoke from the first room." Señor Noah, may I present Habita Mechanico."

A beautiful woman with a sturdy body of no noticeable waist, copper skin, and large almond-shaped black eyes entered." Noah, I'm Habita." Her voice was pleading." Do you remember me?"

Noah felt his gut wrench and his mind inform him that this woman was his sister of the playpen and his mother's schoolroom." Habita, what on earth are you doing here in this house?"

Habita went to Noah, stared into his eyes, and kissed him on each cheek." I married Tomas Mechanico, have a wonderful nine-year-old daughter, and live in this house."

Noah held to her shoulders." Habita, seeing you has ripped my mind open. I cried all the way to Tucson when I was nine years old. My parents took me to other construction projects."

"I thought of you often until I was fourteen. Mama Maru read Doña Sarah's monthly letters to me. She also sent money, but the letters and money stopped suddenly."

"We moved to Chapel Hill about that time. I'm so sorry, but it appears that you were overlooked." Noah paused." I knew nothing of these letters, or the money, but Sarah would think it best to conceal the money from my most thrifty father. Mama Maru, is she alive? We were so lucky to have two wonderful mothers."

"She's alive all right, but not the loving and caring mother we knew. She left me here to shift for myself and wandered all over the Sonora on what she calls a long walk. I worked as a domestic, completed high school, and became a teacher. Mama always was flighty, but she's now a total cuckoo. She's trying to force Roadways and Emblema Compañia to give the old Papago women a reservation. Our Maru now sits along the roadway now with a sour-puss look."

"What happened to her? She was so loving and caring."

"We lost my father, Oidak, in the pit the same time that Doña Sarah's letters, books, and money for my schooling ceased. Maru thought the worse of your parents. Don Josiah and Doña Sarah loved me, spoiling me as terribly as they did you and Josh. And the patrón, Don Josiah, was knowing of the ways of men. Doña Sarah wanted Oidak to have a better job, but Don Josiah let him decide, knowing that Oidak would be shamed by a promotion caused by her. All Papagos envied Maru's friendship with the Chamberlains."

Habita wiped tears from her face." But Maru was mocked by other Papagos for trusting and respecting the Anglos. All enjoyed our loss of money from Doña Sarah. After Oidak's death, they watched with satisfaction as our belongings were thrown from this house, Maru's house, and said Oidak's death was the price of her arrogance."

"How did it become Maru's house?"

"Don Josiah gave it to her when he left Cíbola. Roadways made assurances."

Noah had heard enough of Josiah's praises, reckoning that nine-year-olds wore rosy glasses." We will begin again, Habita. Where do you teach?"

"I taught at the school Doña Sarah started here until Harold and Jorge arrived and dispossessed the Papagos from the mesa. I now teach the best I can at the labor rally point. It's very difficult."

"Where is Tomas now? Does he have work?"

"Tomas is the only Papago from the mesa with work." Habita spoke with pride." He's the boss of all mechanics for the mine's heavy equipment. He returned last night from Nevada where he escorted the last big machine. Harold has promised him work there, but I want him to stay and help our people."

"Mama, I'm back from watching the smiling coyote." A young Indian girl with a notebook clutched in her hand entered the room and stopped when she saw Noah. Her eyes widened when she spied his lucky blue shoes with red laces.

Noah studied her. He was at first puzzled by her appearance and then laughed with disbelief and delight. The girl had her grandmother Maru's features, high cheek bones, sharp nose, and a firm chin.

"Yes, Noah, her resemblance to Maru is remarkable. Her name is Yulla."

Yulla's face registered confusion and then joy." Are you my Tio Noah? Mama told me that you would some day arrive."

"Yes, Yulla, I've come to visit you."

Yulla looked at Habita who gave her a solemn nod of approval. Yulla went to Noah and held her arms up for a hug.

Noah picked her up and hugged perhaps too tightly, for he was not practiced with children. He knew he would never again be free of Cíbola. But at what price? His self-serving mission to come to Cíbola, shut it down, and take his rewards and run was no longer operable.

Noah put Yulla down." Am I to call you Sobrina Yulla, my little niece?"

"No, no, only Yulla. I like the way you say it, but I love to call you Tio." Yulla retrieved her notebook." You are my only Tio, or Tia. Mama and Papa are my only family." Yulla set firm her jaw and squared her shoulders." And my Abuela Maru."

"Where is your Papa, Yulla?"

"He's in his shop just now. He's the best mechanic in the world. What do you do?"

"I'm now to be the best detective in the world." Noah smiled." I'm looking for stolen gold."

"Even a better detective than Columbo?" Yulla was doubtful." Mama lets me watch him on the TV Papa made."

"What work do you want to do, Yulla?"

"Now I'm an apprentice news hound." Yulla removed a stubby pencil from the notebook." I'm going to be a great news hound like Christiane Anmanpour on CNN. She goes everywhere, must have great notes." She opened the notebook. "These notes are on the smiling coyote."

Noah laughed. "Who or what's the smiling coyote, Yulla?"

Yulla frowned. "The smiling coyote is what Abuela Maru calls Emilio the powder man, Rosa's new Apache husband. Emilio always sneaks by to watch Papa work on his side-hill gouger at his workplace out in the maintenance shops. He's a spooky, kooky, powder man, because he's not where he's supposed to be all the time. Sometimes I think I'm watching him, and I turn around and he's watching me. That's spooky."

Noah laughed. "Yulla, you're a clever girl. Do you and your Papa tell Anglos of the side-hill gouger to tease them, something like sending them to the tool room for a left-handed wrench?"

"Don't make jokes about the gouger, Tio Noah. Everyone else does because this is the only machine that won't work for Papa." Yulla lowered her voice to a near whisper. "And the bosses can't know about it because Papa uses their parts and machines to make it. He could get fired, but he can't stop working on it. Mama says he loves the gouger more than her."

"Could we go see this wonderful machine?"

"Of course not, Tio Noah. It's in little pieces and locked in the tool chests." Yulla championed her Papa. "Papa will make the gouger work as soon as he's through with the big machines. I must go now because Emilio is working at his powder bunkers. I'm counting his trips." She dashed from the room.

After chatting further with Habita, Noah returned to the maintenance building. He saw a burly Indian man in the mechanic's work area. He was seated on a metal stool looking at a scattering of metal objects on the floor.

"The gouger?" Noah asked.

The man leaped from the stool as if shot in the butt. "Madre de Dios, you must be Señor Noah Chamberlain. Today, this gouger devil goes to the scrap pile. I'm sorry I kept the contraption."

"Tomas, I've just discovered Habita and Yulla."

Tomas wiped his hands on a cloth and shook Noah's hand, enfolding both of his about Noah's. "Yulla has reported this great event to me. Gracias, muchas gracias, for your kindnesses. I can't repay you." He allowed a shy smile. "Yulla says we are brothers, Tio Noah."

Noah sealed the pact by placing his other hand on the stack. "I would have it no other way. It's very generous of you."

Tomas closed the tool chests that had held gouger parts. "My Papa was what Anglos call a shade tree mechanic in Mexican Nogales. He was the very best at modifying automobiles to cross the border for any purpose. The mafioso drug runners killed him several years ago. I started to build this gouger to honor him. It was to be a dune buggy capable of climbing the walls of the pit."

Noah saw that several framed photographs occupied Tomas' work-bench. A handsome older edition of Tomas in each, buffing or leaning against a vehicle. A matronly woman appeared in one photo.

"Papa was a cactus mechanic as you can see," Tomas said. "That's Mamma. They also killed her when their automobile disappeared in a fireball."

"Don't discard the gouger," Noah said.

"I promised Habita. She's so good and patient. How could she be the daughter of that miserable Maru, who has opposed me always? Papa wanted me to expand the family business, but I had to have Habita. I met her at Imuris looking for Maru who's been wandering around like a crazy woman ever since she lost her house. She refuses to live with us."

"Tell me of the work here at Cíbola," Noah said.

"For many years there was no better job for a Papago in Mexico. Don Carlos convinced Roadways to take a reasonable annual profit from the large ore deposit. Changes for the worse for most Papagos started when Harold raided us." Tomas gazed at the floor. "And I became a whore, lusting to work on the new heavy equipment. I've begged Harold for a job in Nevada, but Habita is trying to shame me into staying here and fighting for the dispossessed Papagos' homes. And now Maru prowls the roadway to the mesa babbling about a Brother Cuckoo savior who will return the mesa to the dispossessed Papagos."

Tomas looked up and smiled. "Are you, the son of the great Don Josiah, bound for Cíbola to be Maru's Brother Cuckoo savior?"

"Not me. I was sent here by the man you call the great Don Josiah to sell all valuables left on the mesa and then slink away, leaving the Papagos with nothing, hardly a savior's work. But now I've been instructed to determine first if Victor has actually suffered a theft of any gold due him. Can you assist me?"

"From its earliest days, Cíbola excited each of us to believe that we would discover and possess a fist-sized nugget that would make us rich, but this isn't possible in this ore deposit. The gold is micron flakes with only a few nuggets encrusted in worthless rock. You would have to steal a dump truck load of the micron ore to have enough gold to buy only a transmission for your beautiful black automobile."

"Does that mean that theft could only be possible starting with the leaching process?"

Tomas laughed. "Not likely, Noah, unless the thief wished to bathe in cyanide solutions. The gold slurry isn't safe until melted and molded into impure bars for shipment to refiners. The gold wagon guards always stood ready to receive these very large bars."

"Under whose surveillance?"

"Jorge, always Jorge, for he's the only person at Cíbola all trusted, as do I. Jorge would never do anything so stupid as to take gold from his own operations. Catalans are very prudent."

"You've eliminated all suspects then, Tomas. I can report to Josiah that no thefts have occurred and work with you and Habita to help the Papagos reclaim their homes."

"It isn't possible for me to stay here for, I'm bound for Nevada. Meanwhile, I must be loyal to Harold. Perhaps Habita will follow me, but she's her mother's daughter." Tomas tidied his work area. "You should consider one other gold theft possibility. Many banditos have gathered at Libertad. Couldn't they hold up the gold wagon on its way to Hermosillo, threatening the guards' lives if they didn't give them a gold bar, or a portion, from time to time?"

"If so, it's not my concern," Noah said. "I'm not responsible for outside incidents. Anyway, I now believe all claims of gold theft are just wild rumors intended to make mischief for the Anglos. I'll bet the locals are having a lot of laughs at my expense."

"Laughter at you is much preferred to fear, as they feel for Harold. A man who is feared by many has many to fear. Papagos are waiting to

see if you're Don Josiah's son. He and Don Carlos were much respected
by the elders."

Noah rejected anything that deified Josiah. The poor Papagos on this
mesa were easily impressed by regular wages, providing them with
water, food, and shelter. What more, after all, had really been done for
them by Don Josiah? He deserted them and never looked back, a greedy
man doing the bidding of big-business big shots.

"My father has unfortunately not lived up to his myth," Noah said.
"I don't admire him or his work. I'm here only to please Ludie."

Tomas glanced at the picture of his father and mother. "I, too, differed
with my father. I wish he had survived, so I could seek reconciliation.
Work has become too great a part of our lives."

"Is Victor trusted and respected by the Papagos? Have they given
him a free pass as Don Carlos' son?"

"No, no, for they observe that he is only another Spaniard in Mexican
clothing seeking gold. The old Papago women have revived the story of
the Spanish conquistadores pursuit of pyrite, fools gold, many miles to
the east of Cíbola. The legend tells of forty-three Spaniards who per-
ished of thirst in that place almost three hundred years ago while following their Papago slave into what the Spaniards called the despoblado, the awful, deadly deserted wilderness. They called the slave
Pendejo because of his cuckoo ways. The conquistador masters likened
this poor man to a bawdy, good-for-nothing fool. But Pendejo was a
gifted orator when he spoke of the great golden heaps of treasure that
existed in the heart of the despoblado, surely the Seven Cities of Cíbola.
Pendejo led them there and vanished, yet another Brother Cuckoo trickster. This place of false splendor is named Pendejos Punto for the forty-
three Spaniard pendejos who followed him and died of thirst while
wandering in circles in the despoblado."

Yulla entered the shop area, notebook in hand and a perplexed look
in her eyes. "Tio Noah, Emilio is now more kooky than spooky. He runs

his loaded machine up and down the pit road hauling powder both ways. He will never finish his chores that way. Is he now cuckoo?"

"Cuckoo like a coyote, Yulla." Noah took her hand. "Let's go to Rosa's lunchroom, and I'll explain the art of make-work. Your Papa will get your Mama and join us. Then you can tell me how Columbo captures spooky-kooky gold banditos who leave no clues and forget to steal the gold."

# Chapter 4

Tuesday morning, Noah set out on an early-morning, five-mile run to Cíbola's south rim. He was pleased that his conditioning allowed him to run at a sprightly gait. His view of the desert floor from the path along the south rim stirred memories of the magical place of his childhood. Unfortunately, the north rim man-made badlands prevented a run circling the mesa.

Yesterday evening, Noah had run to the north rim, following the large water pipeline until it plunged over the side of the mesa on its downward path to the desert floor. Below, the pipeline ended in a fenced enclosure, surely the wellhead for the deep water well. Beyond the fenced enclosure, the shrine-site now called Libertad was visible, marked by a sprinkling of electric lights and many cook fires. Behind a jumble of buildings, Noah detected an area that, from his vantage point, resembled the old Roman amphitheater in Tarragona, Spain.

But this morning, without the ugly marks of man, the vast desert flowing to the horizon in the south justified the praise Maru gave it, and to her Papago people. "We call ourselves O'odham, the People," she had said. "We are descended from those ancients, the Hohokums, who emerged from the dry sands." Maru had always spoken with focus and clarity when she proclaimed that Papagos are the earth itself in a land of little rain. That, she had made known to Noah, was the secret, the essence, of their lives. Papagos, the desert people, love and revere their land. Only outsiders consider it to be a despoblado.

Noah related these concepts to Jorge, asking what right did outsiders have to violate this balance? Jorge asserted that a superb gold deposit was to be mined with maximum efficiency, because that's what being a mine engineer was all about. He wasn't responsible for the deposit existing in the middle of a despoblado that stupid people insist on living in.

On the home stretch back to the guesthouse, Noah approached the gate. A trooper new to Noah watched him from the gatehouse door, reluctant to enter the mounting heat.

Chiricahua peered from the roof lookout station above the gatehouse. "Bueno, Perez, I'll receive Señor Noah. Perhaps he wishes to join me."

Noah climbed to the roof and noted a cot under a covered section by the head-high parapet. "I see you have assistance. Does it go well?"

"Of course not. I've been here since Saturday. Captain Guardia has assigned Perez, who is always dour, here during his scheduled holiday. He complains to me because I allow the old women to cluster before the gates and give them water."

"An Apache does this for Papagos?"

"We all have grandmothers."

"Are the old women the grandmothers of those dispossessed from Cíbola by Jorge?"

"Sí, but they're joined by other dispossessed old women from throughout the Sonora. Some are Apaches."

Noah was eager to take advantage of the now-chatty sergeant. "Por favor, may I ask you a question about the gold wagon guards when they delivered gold?"

"You're attempting to interrogate me concerning their fate?"

"My superior in Chapel Hill ordered me to determine if there was a gold theft."

"My superior in Hermosillo instructed you in my presence to leave the gold theft investigation to the Federales. You're Señor Inside, he's Señor Outside."

"Guardia is sporting with me, telling me nothing about the investigation."

Chiricahua placed his visored cap on a table and replaced it with a twisted red bandana. "Why don't you accept that the gold wagon guards are guilty? This is an insult to Captain Guardia."

"I observe too many coincidences. Why were they snatched away just as I arrived and Victor departed?"

Chiricahua walked to the edge of the roof to assure that Perez remained indoors. "I'll answer one question only if you answer one for me. These exchanges of confidences remain on this roof."

"Done. Your question?"

"Why does Captain Guardia order me and Perez to protect you?"

"Probably because he considers me to be inept and my replacement would be troublesome to him."

Chiricahua nodded judiciously. "And now your question."

"Why won't Guardia let me leave the mesa if I'm too inept to cope with my assignment? What harm can I do him?"

"You would not survive, and he would be blamed by Señor Victor for harming his negotiations with Ludie Carter. Captain Guardia's a shrewd man when it suits his purposes." Chiricahua's ever-alert eyes shifted to the roadway.

Following Chiricahua's gaze, Noah saw an oversized van on massive tires lumbering up to the gate. Without prompting, Perez drove a military vehicle's front bumper to the inside gate bar and inserted a rocket launcher device through an opening in the gate. Chiricahua brought a large rifle from a locked closet behind the cot.

"Por favor, lower your head, Señor Noah." Chiricahua's voice was calm. "Often mafioso drug runners favor such vehicles."

The van pulled up to within six feet of the gate and an Indian man got out. "Hola, Señor Noah Chamberlain, if you please. Tell him Francisco Vásquez of Libertad wishes to visit with him on a business matter of importance."

"Do you wish to speak to this man?" Chiricahua asked. "He makes and sells survival tools to migrants at Libertad."

"Let me go speak with him, and keep the van outside the gate."

Chiricahua nodded with satisfaction and motioned Perez to make a man opening only at the gate. "Please assure that the van holds no explosives. If you've doubts, call me."

Noah exited through the gate and shook Francisco's extended hand. "Hola, so you've a business at Libertad?"

A smile further broadened Francisco's copper face, bracketed by battered, protruding ears. He spoke in English. "I'm the only legitimate business down there." He tugged an orange and black-billed cap to a jaunty position. "I've evolved from a college jock-strap to a tycoon. You're in the presence of a two-time NCAA wrestling champion at one hundred and sixty-seven pounds." He bowed from the waist. "Idaho State University in Pocatello, Idaho, ten years ago, thank you very much."

"May I see your van?" Noah asked. "Your engine was as if on idle while you approached."

"It would be my pleasure." Francisco led Noah to the van. "After college graduation, I was a shop teacher for five years. This van's a composite of twenty different vehicles and a hundred class projects. The motor is a diesel from a truck, with modifications."

Noah was interested in a fellow teacher. He received a detailed guided tour of the mini-shop, trying to ask questions that Francisco considered worthy of answers. All equipment crammed into the van was sparkling clean.

"After they closed down my shop classes to cut school budgets in

Pocatello, I used the van to start a fix-it business on wheels." Francisco shrugged. "The Anglos there didn't favor a forgotten sports hero who drank too much firewater and gained forty pounds, a real boozy lard-ass. My customers and my Anglo wife bailed out. Too damn bad because I found my real thing is being a craftsman."

Francisco jumped from the van and pointed to one of the water towers. "Now for the good news. I've come to buy that water tower from you for Libertad West. And water from the well at the mesa base to keep it filled. Can we talk?"

"We can talk if you leave that pistol in your belt in the van." Noah led the way through the gate and to a water tower. "Is this your first time at Cíbola?"

"No. I applied for work here a couple of years ago shortly after arriving in the Sonora and lasted a couple of days on the labor gang. They didn't need my specialties and had me pushing a broom in the maintenance building. Shortly after that, I went into business at Libertad."

Francisco examined the leaching and neighboring melting facilities with care. "Look how well maintained this equipment is after several years of use, no under-maintenance here to cut costs." He gazed up at the water tower. "Same deal on this baby. Could it be mine?"

"I would like to help you, so I'll check it out with Roadways. I've seen other shrine sites. What kind of shoddy shrine goods do you make?"

"Please, nothing shoddy in my stalls. Survival, not pseudo religious solutions, is my business. Come to Libertad and see my survival utensils. I make solar stoves, cooking utensils, and agricultural tools. Other stuff is on the drawing board."

"What are you going to do if you can't get water?"

"I've diddled around with Plan A, and Plan B, and Plan C. Plan A is to get out of the shrine site into a Libertad West with well water. Plan B says I take my ill-gotten gains back to Pocatello and rub noses in them."

"What's Plan C?"

Francisco brightened. "Plan C is to turn legitimate as a shop teacher —entrepreneur in a place about eight hundred miles south of here I call Tres Rios. I'll start a school – Tres Rios Escuela – to train the poor folk down there to be craftspeople. Plenty of willing, unemployed hands are there with great potential. And there are three rivers that come tumbling out of mountains so high they make Mt. Borah look like a spud cellar. I've been there three times because the lasses even think I'm sexy. Statues of their resident god have bat-wing ears – must have been a serious wrestler also."

He couldn't control his enthusiasm. "People would stay at home down there if they had jobs to survive. It's a shame because they've got water up to their armpits and trees galore to build houses. You know, if I went down there, I would be a hard working, survival utensil-making guy. Come down and take a look sometime."

"I'll come after I get a 'get out of jail' pass from Guardia. What would you do at a Libertad West?"

Francisco noted the sun's position to check the time of day. "I'm not good at shrine site stuff. I just want to make and sell my survival utensils. My best shot is to move my shop a mile west of the sick playground Libertad has become." He fingered one of his ears. "We all have big ears down at Libertad. What's a Roadways' big-shot's son doing at Cíbola?"

"I'm a teacher, too, on kind of an unscheduled sabbatical."

"Where was your last gig?"

"Way down south of here. We were doing special classes teaching Indian-speaking people of all ages to speak and write Spanish and English. The idea was to provide them with the language tools to deal with any work situation in all the Americas." Noah shrugged. "Well, they might want to stay out of Montreal."

"Are you the Noah of the Noah's Ark Escuela that was near the village of Comitan in Chiapas?"

Noah nodded.

"Hot damn, you are for sure. It's an honor to meet you, Brother, but from what I hear you might want to keep a low profile in the Sonora for a while. Storm troopers hate it when the villagers man the walls and fight with rocks and sticks." Francisco pointed to the housing area. "May I prowl that juicy junk heap across the road before I leave? I'm into alchemy down at Libertad, turning scrap into survival items for gold."

Noah executed the high-five Francisco offered. "I see room for barter, so you come back soon. I dare you to pocket a bolt and see if you get it by the sergeant. I'm betting on him."

"No way, not that one." Francisco smiled weakly. "I thought the Shoshone were bad-asses, but that Apache makes me want to stay in the tipi with the women."

Noah returned to Chiricahua at the gate. "I authorized Francisco to examine the scrap heap. He makes and sells survival utensils for migrant workers crossing the Arizona border for jobs."

"Francisco does that well," Chiricahua said. "A pity he doesn't control all of Libertad."

As Noah returned to the maintenance building, he saw Francisco standing transfixed before Intimidator parked by the guest house. He then circled the huge machine, fingertips of his right hand caressing its black surface.

* * *

Perez escorted Wayne Coffer, Josiah's financial whiz, to Noah's office at mid-morning. Noah shook the hand the stocky, ruddy-faced man offered him before they were seated, and then he closed the door to prevent the unwanted access of Emilio.

"I appreciate you doing this for me, Wayne," Noah said. "Sorry for the crazy schedule, but they've got me bottled up on this mesa."

Wayne placed a battered briefcase on the large desk that otherwise held only a plate containing corn cake crumbs. "I'm glad for the assignment from Josiah. I'm only sixty-five years old, but my wife is ailing and wanted to move out to Fearrington Village. We're luckier than most folks, because my Roadways pension will suit us fine unless something real bad happens to our health. A little double-dipping is good for our cash flow."

"Josiah said that you're cleared for all rumors, lies, and even the truth."

"I would do about anything for Big Josiah. He dug me out of a caved-in trench once when everyone else had given up on me. Josiah said this was on the quiet, so I'll keep things to myself."

"This is not quite as cloak-and-dagger as it appears. But you know how obsessed with contingency planning Josiah's always been. He sent me here to shut this place down, but the gold theft flap's heated up. So I'm looking for information on why Victor is so convinced that he's been ripped off."

"Josiah's contingency plan told him where to dig for me, and his radar tells him something's out of balance down here. Watch your wallet in this job. Harold's a slick operator, one of my steady customers when I headed the internal audits department. And we're old buddies at Emblema Compania headquarters in Mexico City. Those guys wrote the book on cooking the books."

Wayne gazed at a mine map on the wall. "Cíbola's the best designed mining and ore processing facility on the planet, thanks to Jorge. He also executed the most god-awful destruction of a local workforce's rights imaginable, thanks to Harold."

"Did Grethe endorse this all the way?"

"Grethe was a model of ignorance and apathy. She didn't know what was happening here, and she didn't care. Grethe, above all else, wanted to placate Harold and make him look good to her board of directors and Ludie."

"Was Cíbola profitable?" Noah asked.

"Outstanding, really outstanding. Jorge took more than one hundred million dollars worth of gold out of here in three years, and their costs were rock bottom. An excellent precious metal recovery rate is ninety-three percent, but Jorge's design beat that, unbelievable. It's never been done before on an ore body like this one, a real bitch-kitty."

"So Anglo greed did run amok here."

"Totally out of control, you bet," Wayne said. "The shame is that the technology was so good that workers could've been treated first-class. Four gold wagon guards should have been plenty, but destruction of worker loyalty made theft so common that the guard force was doubled, and Jorge had to spend half his time being the security czar. An hour of non-productive time each shift was spent searching all workers so they couldn't steal gloves, small tools, or toilet paper."

"Was there gold theft?"

"No way. That was the area Jorge really hammered away at. He finally gave up the supervision of gate searches and took complete control of the gold recovery area."

"So Victor started complaining that he wasn't getting his full measure of the gold shortly after Jorge arrived?"

"You bet, loud and often," Wayne said. "The guard force called it preventive bitching and moaning. Jorge treated those gold bars they ferried to Hermosillo like, well, gold bars." He opened his briefcase and removed a single sheet of paper. "I've got to tell you that the distribution of profits from this operation was entirely in order, unbelievable. Who would think it with Harold and Victor involved? Not me, no siree." He tapped the bottom of the page. "And what's more unbelievable is that this operation's productivity, low costs, and fiscal accountability set an industry high standard."

Noah took the sheet of paper and stared at it. "I hoped you would dig up some dirt for me that would give me some leverage down here. I do my best when I'm winging it. I hoped I could come to Cíbola and be my own man."

Wayne rubbed his right knuckles with his left thumb. "Kind of wish I could stay here, but Josiah said get in and out fast-like, or Ludie would jump on him."

Noah now understood why Josiah considered Wayne worth digging for. "Why is Victor so intent on making an issue about this worthless property?"

"Cíbola's problems are his chance to get back on a footing with Roadways that Don Carlos established when Lisbeth ran the show. Emblema Compañia greased the palms of Mexican authorities to win prime road construction projects for Roadways Company, receiving thirty percent of the net profits while risking no capital monies. Damn nice work if you can get it."

"I'm not even performing well on the gold theft investigation." Noah slumped in his chair. "I'm not cut out for this crisis intervention stuff, never have been. I've got to do things my own way."

"Then you should've turned the assignment down. You're Josiah's substitute, so you have to follow the Roadways' paradigm. Upward mobility can be achieved only by defeating all the roadblocks placed in your path. You can't just visit an organization and play a few hands in their game, no dabblers allowed."

Noah straightened in the chair. "Following the paradigm sounds like a Star Trek episode. Are we talking about the same thing here? I'm only on a temporary assignment to close the gates on this place and lose Josiah again."

"Unfortunately, I'm all too certain. My son, Johnny, was five years older than you. He also dedicated himself to distancing himself from me and my dedication to succeed in big business by trying really hard.

He claimed that I fought for promotions just to be a big shot, not accepting that I had to fight to make the leaders share more of the property I was helping them acquire. Working for others is always about distribution of property. I had a family to support and was getting peanuts."

"What's wrong with being a worker?" Noah lost interest in a conversation now becoming an assertive sermon sounding too much like Josiah's. "Was that too demeaning?"

Wayne didn't back off. "No, Noah, the entry work was fine, except for the low pay, but it became intolerable when the co-workers selected to be my bosses were constantly on my case, because they realized my professional capabilities were greater than theirs and tried to put me down. I figured that it was either eat their crap, be pushed out the back door, or go up the career ladder. Are you listening to me, Noah?"

He waited for Noah to make eye contact. "Every big business organization has an internal assertive crisis intervention paradigm put in place by leaders to ensure that their followers constantly battle to improve themselves and, in turn, the organization's capabilities to defeat competitor organizations. It's called the survival of the fittest, Noah. If you're not content to stay with the bottom feeders, you must engage in the internal combats."

"That sounds ugly to me," Noah said. "I did the right thing by escaping Josiah as soon as I could and devoting my time to work that doesn't require this stupid model."

"Unfortunately, I understand what you're saying all too well. You want to do something of value for people who're so needy and vulnerable they're grateful for your tiniest contributions. No assertive paradigm exists because the work is so lacking in financial rewards that no one's competing for it. Doing good with no hassle just feels good. Right?"

"You're damn right it does! If it's done right, there's no direct confrontation needed. I learned a hard lesson in Chiapas, too ambitious.

Next time I'll be more unobtrusive."

"If it's an unobtrusive life without confrontation you want, you can go to a monastery, or, God forbid, take the path my Johnny took. He disappeared into a commune in the Netherlands with nothing but a backpack and was carried out three years later dead from an overdose of heroin. Johnny's journey scared the hell out of Josiah, so he kept tabs on you to see if you needed support. He's afraid of the price you may be willing to pay to remain a maverick."

"But Josiah ruined our relationship with his constant intrusive scrutiny."

Wayne signed deeply. "That's his way alright. He's always been hell-bent to risk everything to win everything. Tell you what, Noah. I wish Johnny's feelings were injured instead of his body beyond repair. The pity of it is that I could've saved him if I had been willing to use my assertive crisis intervention skills. He wanted his space and I gave it to him, against my better judgment. We old geezers can't win nowadays. I failed Johnny as a father, and you've convinced Josiah that he's failed you. He, at least, gave it his best shots."

"Did Josiah send you to Cíbola to help me or lecture me? Help's appreciated, but long-winded lectures only piss me off. Just put your crisis intervention thinking cap on and clue me in."

"Fair enough," Wayne said. "For me, things are kind of clear-cut down here at Cíbola. Harold savaged these folks, and they want revenge on him before Roadways withdraws. Their native cunning tells them that a crisis can be an opportunity for them. It could be for you, too, if you'll get on the ball. Josiah didn't invent crisis intervention, so don't shun the methods to show your displeasure with the man."

Wayne's words, meant to reassure Noah, gave him momentary near panic. What if he did accept Josiah's thinking and buy into the Don Josiah legend? Unthinkable. "I can't wait to get this assignment behind me, so I can get back to teaching where I belong."

"I hope that's soon because things are happening too fast in Mexico nowadays. I'm bugging out of here to the good old US of A right now. By now, the Federales' computers have spotted me, and it's best that Victor doesn't get his hands on me. And you can bet your boots that the goons from Chiapas will be here sooner or later. As you've learned the hard way, they're damned hard to avoid."

Noah now understood that Josiah had changed his assignment to the gold theft quagmire only as a red herring luring him away from doing battle with Harold and Victor. He decided to use Wayne – surely a part of Josiah's surveillance network – to resolve the gold theft issue without encountering direct confrontation. It would be gratifying to teach two old watchdogs some new tricks.

* * *

Chiricahua was at his habitual post on the gatehouse roof when Noah and Emilio arrived in Intimidator with their curious cargo six hours after Wayne's departure. Chiricahua observed as Noah prepared for Guardia's arrival. At first, he remained on the roof, but he soon returned to ground level and approached the linen covered table that Emilio set with the silver coffee service.

Noah put on his suit jacket and made a minute adjustment to his necktie. His big shot formal wardrobe, Noah thought, one suit, one necktie, and one white shirt. The lucky blue shoes with red laces would have to do. To compensate, he had shaved his beard and received an excellent haircut from Rosa. It was showtime.

Noah repositioned the two ornate chairs from the hospitality room. "May I assist you, Sergeant?"

Chiricahua lifted the tablecloth and peered under the table. "Do you have guns?"

"No guns for me, ever."

"You're fortunate to have the luxury of choice."

"Are you going to disarm everyone on the mesa?"

"No need, for those with guns are known to me, and my captain can care for himself. I only protect against a surprise, because he underestimates you."

When a horn sounded at the gate, Perez admitted Guardia driving a Federales vehicle, accompanied by one trooper. A second vehicle remained outside the gate.

Guardia approached with a smile. "Hola, Señor Inside, so it's good news you have for me? I thought so from your hurried telephone call."

As soon as they were seated, Noah tugged his left earlobe to cue Habita with the video camera. "Actually, Guardia, I've good news and bad news for you. You'll be pleased to learn that I've solved the gold theft riddle." He saluted Guardia with his coffee cup. "You may now release the gold wagon guards from your hasty arrest. As I speak, we're celebrating this happy news inside Cíbola."

"And the bad news?" Guardia removed his hat and lazed back in his chair.

"You're out of work here, Señor Outside. We need no police at Cíbola because no gold was stolen. Claims of a theft were all a rumor to slander Roadways, so now Chiricahua and Perez may depart."

Guardia looked at the gate. "You would have me leave the rat hole unguarded while still hunting rats? What if you're wrong and five million dollars in gold was stolen?"

"We'll take care of ourselves. I'll bet my life on it."

"Of course you will, and the lives of others. What of Habita and Rosa and the little girl, Yulla? What convinces you to endanger their lives?"

Noah removed a videocassette from his jacket pocket. "I've joined the news hound legions and recorded the testimony of a noted international internal auditor, Wayne Coffer. After an exhaustive investigation in Mexico, Canada, and the United States, he certifies that no gold thefts whatsoever have occurred. "

Guardia replaced his hat. "Then this is a news hound event also?"

"It would seem so."

"Por favor, give me the video." Guardia received the cassette on his outstretched palm. "You possess other copies?"

"It would seem so."

"But your video will be pathetic and not be believed in a court of law."

"It would seem so, but the dispossessed are eager to believe that the Federales are capable of all outrages. The video will be as popular as the cock fights."

"Thank you, Señor Inside, for returning me to familiar ground, blackmail. You, like Harold, hide greed and treachery behind affable Anglo manners. What's your price?"

Noah replenished their coffee and allowed himself a moment of self-congratulations. "Instruct Victor to quit harassing my efforts to shut down Cíbola, and inform the old Papago women that Harold no longer directs Cíbola, so they'll abandon their blockade. No more."

Guardia come to attention in his chair. "Bueno. I'm in full accord with you and appear at Cíbola at this time on my own volition to assist the Emblema Compañia in their untiring efforts to assist the good people of the Sonora." His elocution was admirable. "All assistance will be given to hasten Roadways early, secure exit from the Sonora."

"That is very satisfactory, Señor Outside." Noah again tugged his left earlobe.

Guardia glanced at Habita seated on the porch of the dilapidated general store, camera on the ready. "You've never dealt with crime or criminals, have you?"

"Only to run from them."

"So a major theft to you is a business inconvenience. For me, it's a puzzle to be solved to capture a criminal. Each crime committed in my jurisdiction, be it a stolen goat or a fatal stabbing in a cantina, has a victim and one or more suspects. And the alibis are truly works of art. Assault crimes are committed in a place where I find a dead body or an injured victim who's harmed by a weapon. And clues can be anything and everywhere. Do you know a clue when you see one?"

Noah tried to recall Josiah's lecture. He said things like clues will point to various suspects and will eventually produce a solution. A clue can be physical evidence, body language, or unguarded comments; and they can build and work in pairs and trios. But how about false clues that point to the wrong suspect? He made an offer. "Clues, of course, are those pieces of evidence that were leading me to suspect the gold guards, but they were uncovered as false."

"Tell me, Señor Inside, how you have managed to blind yourself to the obvious? Thievery is afoot at Cíbola. I'll provide proof in due course in the proper venue. For now, I've a much greater crisis to confront in the Sonora."

Noah decided a modicum of righteous indignation was indicated, because this wasn't the finale he envisioned. Where were Guardia's gracious handshake, profuse thanks, and hasty departure? "The people deserve to know of your activities. Have you other suspects?" He started sweating, removing his jacket as if it were the cause.

"Very well. I suspect Habita and Tomas, Rosa and Emilio, and, of course, Jorge and Harold. I am investigating the backgrounds of all. For instance, Emilio is an excellent powder man, but also a small-time Don Juan trickster. Leisure time's the only time he flirts with trouble. Por favor, do us both a favor and quit your detective efforts."

"I can't. Roadways won't let me."

"Then tell them that the best sleuth in all Mexico, myself, has been on the case from the beginning. Forgive me, but the theft of gold is of no consequence compared to the major drug smuggling network I must destroy. I was sent to the Sonora to do this thing. You are now impeding this long, complex investigation by your failure to close this facility and leave the Sonora quickly."

Noah, feeling hot and ridiculous, ripped off his necktie. "You didn't do anything until Victor showed up and I arrived. A typical save-your-own-ass maneuver." Guardia couldn't hide the punch scored. "You spent too much time showing off for Victor, like sending him back to Hermosillo in your military vehicle. Don't you dare suggest that Habita or Tomas are thieves. They're wonderful people, the salt of the earth." He enjoyed flailing away at Guardia so much he failed to note that he was no longer landing blows.

Guardia stood and looked down on Noah. "Sergeant Chiricahua tells me of an old Papago woman called Maru who tells a Great-Grandmother myth foretelling of a Papago Brother Cuckoo savior who will destroy the Apaches. You, Tio Noah, have embraced a dreadful family sworn to kill me, Chiricahua, and Perez, their only hope for survival. Chiricahua and Perez will return to the safety of the outside with me now."

Noah leaped up and, in a fit of frustration, shoved over Guardia's chair. "I'm coming to Hermosillo tomorrow morning for the four guards. We'll see how the news hounds report my journey for justice."

Guardia righted the chair. "Come if you wish. You'll make my day. But, Señor Inside, this isn't a checkmate for you. The contest will end only by your banishment from Mexico, hopefully before your incarceration or death."

# Chapter 5

A fitful night, featuring another Chiapas nightmare, convinced Noah to go to Guardia's lair in Hermosillo and press for the release of the gold guards. Thus far, he had been too content to play the neutral Mr. Inside role. Staying penned-up and trying to follow orders wasn't at all maverick-like. He decided on a "he-can't-find-me, he can't-bug-me" policy with Josiah and left Tomas in charge of gate security. Locating the prison was easy, the most prosperous enterprise in the dusty town located in a sprawling, high-walled, adobe building. Waiting for Guardia all morning outside his barracks-like office gave Noah added, unneeded, instruction in the treatment of the underclass in Mexico. The hair on the back of his neck rose each time he heard someone call out in the tomb-like structure. Finally, he was permitted to enter Guardia's office.

Guardia was dismissive, recognizing an ex-big shot groping for a way to cling to the survival ladder. "I'm not impressed by anything your fellow Anglo, Wayne, has to say. He professes to be an unimpeachable auditor of accounts, but he who walks among the coyotes learns to howl."

"But I'm certain that no gold has been stolen." Noah wasn't offered a seat. "The old Papago women's blockade is the real problem, so make them go away and I will vacate Cíbola in a few days. Let me take the gold guards back with me now to calm things down."

"So you wish to strike a bargain with me?" None of the coffee Guardia sipped was offered to Noah. "Bueno. We now have done a deal. I've already arranged for the release of the four guards. They depart from Mexico today, and so must you."

Removing a file from a drawer and centering it on his otherwise barren desk, Guardia shocked Noah into silence. "Noah Chamberlain, I've actually been trying to prevent your arrest by my Federales compatriots in Chiapas. Yes, I know of the problems you encountered there and advise you, regardless of the injustices you suffered, to return to the United States as soon as possible. It appears that your video of our palaver on the mesa was placed in the hands of the news hounds after all. Do yourself a favor and disappear from the Sonora before you're swept away by the white-gold wars, cocaina. I'll take a force to Cíbola for a rat hunt one day soon. For now, you must scurry back to the United States."

Stunned by the fluidity of the Sonora's sandy playing fields and the absence of fair play, Noah felt an urgent need to flee the stronghold of the Federales. He must now tell Ludie that he had failed on his temporary assignment, not an auspicious beginning for a consort. As he escaped the prison gate, a beat-up rental car parked one space from Intimidator.

Harold got out of the vehicle with a smirk of delight. "As I live and breathe, here's Junior Chamberlain, the crack Cíbola director. Are you lost, Junior?"

Noah hated Harold's haughty manner, but he loved that his fifty years were evident, especially the sparse blond hair, long strands forced to do extra, winding duty across a balding head. When Harold removed his safari jacket and turned to puzzle over the prison signs, Noah was delighted to see a gusset in the rear of his pants. Old Harold was becoming a porker.

"And here is Harold, the ex-everything." Noah said. "Please tell me that you are here to mend fences with me. No, I suppose not. The Anglo and the Saxon in you doesn't permit bending, especially in those britches."

Harold went into a tight-lipped, hands-on-hips act of royal indignation, very satisfying. "Ludie is stupid for interfering in a well-executed business campaign. What a farce it is to allow Josiah to send you down here, Junior! But I will soon convince her to pluck you out of the Sonora and send you on your way to the next gigolo assignment."

"Wishful thinking, Harold. You go in and face the gold guards. I'm bound for Cíbola to tidy up."

"What a simpleton," Harold said. "You're history, Junior, and so is that faithful fool, Josiah. The gold guards are being released to me, and my plane departs from Hermosillo in an hour. We'll all sleep in our beds in Toronto tonight. I'll soon be back to fire Jorge to appease Victor because often sacrifices of even your best troops must be made to stay on a winning path."

\* \* \*

As Intimidator thundered back to Cíbola, Noah called Ludie at Roadways' headquarters three times on his cellular phone, but she refused to accept his calls. Finally, in desperation, he called Josiah who responded to his call immediately.

Josiah's voice was uncharacteristically tentative as he read a letter from Ludie to Noah, mumbled something about how sorry he was for Noah, and transferred the call to Ludie.

"Thanks for finally accepting my call, Ludie." Noah did his utmost to calm his voice. "I've got the message from Josiah and will sure as hell get out of your life. I'm damned lucky to escape the crafty Carter clan."

"So noted," Ludie said. "No harm, no foul. Is that it? I've got a real full calendar today." She sounded as if she were dismissing a bellhop.

"No, not so noted. And don't think that I'm still lusting after your ass. I get a certified letter from you announcing in two legalese lines that our engagement is null and void. That's great stuff, Ludie. We moved from marriage plans to final divorce procedures without going through the middle touchy-feely stuff."

Ludie said nothing, but he could hear her take a deep breath.

Noah was furious at her silence. "The last time I was with you I was awarded a lusty bounce on the sofa. I was making love, and you were having recreational sex with a family retainer, the retarded son of your chamberlain. Was I that bad as a lover?" He desperately wanted to escape this moment.

"I had to make a public break from you," Ludie said. "Grethe left the company to me, but with the stipulation that Harold must approve my marriage partner. I pretended we were engaged to buy some time. Besides, you needed money and Josiah wanted you to return to Cíbola." She took another deep breath. "I had to do it for my Great-Grandmother Mariah and Roadways."

"I'll get out of Chapel Hill, so you can get on with your life – conniving and sporting with the hired hands." Noah was yelling into the phone.

"Grow up, Noah," Ludie said, "Having sex was your idea, and so I decided to finish some old high school business. You seem to have performance anxieties, so let me assure you that I enjoyed the sex immensely, but your performance at Cíbola shows that you don't belong in the same league with Josiah." She disconnected the call.

For several miles, Noah punished Intimidator's steering wheel with his pounding fist. Whoever said pride comes before the fall got it right, he thought. He knew all too well that Grethe and her predecessors had built Roadways Company by using cunning – intervening in crises by devious, indirect means. They had mastered the art of influencing and controlling opponents, so that desired results were achieved without direct confrontations. Beautiful. His overestimation of himself as a stud had made him a pawn in a power game he wasn't qualified to play in. How malleable can a guy be?

He longed to go off-road and let the big machine lose them in the despoblado, but his anger and survival instincts saved him. His prime chore now was to keep out of the clutches of the Chiapas Federales. Noah called Jorge to give him the news that Harold was once more in command, but might barter him away also.

Jorge answered his phone on the first ring, and listened without comment as Noah also told him of his rejection by Ludie. "Noah, I have also been informed by Ludie that I am unfit to serve her. I must leave Cíbola immediately, for I have been terminated at the insistence of Victor and Harold. I not only cannot be a manager in Nevada, but also I am denied my patents pending on three major innovations I invented for the melting processes."

"Jorge, I'm so sorry," Noah said. "How can I help you?"

"Perhaps we can help each other. Hurry back to Cíbola, for I have a most promising proposal for you."

\* \* \*

"What's the deal, Jorge?" Noah was in desperate need of positive news as he stood in Jorge's office door. "Give me some clues."

"I am now free to do as I please. Clues are that our project will be very lucrative, and a balance of power will be restored when we claim another gold deposit to the east. As we speak, Emilio is packing all your belongings in my truck, and Rosa is preparing food and drink for a most rewarding journey. Come quickly to the maintenance shop."

While Tomas topped off the large blue truck's fuel tanks, Noah studied the maps given to him by Jorge. He scanned the route across the despoblado from Cíbola to the Arizona border. The route was not direct because of the need to follow a road in a rift that skirted bad lands directly to the north. They were to travel east and turn north at a gap in the rift identified as Pendejos Punto. Noah gave Tomas a backslap and got into the passenger's seat.

Noah had completed his farewells to Habita and Yulla amid considerable tears, his as well as theirs. All were assured that he was accompanying Jorge on a gold prospecting journey to the east, soon to return. Tomas assured that he would guard the gate until Harold's arrival, furthering his cause for a job in Nevada.

"Let's do it, Jorge," Noah said. "Damn, we've lost the daylight."

Jorge chuckled. "That is the idea. We must pass between the well and Libertad to get to the rift road." He eased the big vehicle down the roadway from Cíbola, beeping the truck's horn at the crowds of old Papago women. "Why do you bother guarding Cíbola?"

"If someone else occupies it, they may harm Yulla and her parents," Noah said.

A short distance beyond the labor rallying area, Jorge turned on a rutted road that circled the mesa to Libertad. He took a gun from a basket between the seats and placed it in his lap. "Libertad is beyond the next ridge. We will need some luck to get through undetected."

"Why didn't you shutdown Libertad long ago?" Noah asked. "Guardia told me that it's a rats nest of drug traffickers, coyote migrant smugglers, and con artists."

"Harold and I decided that a modicum of support of Libertad was a fair exchange for a facility that siphoned away the dispossessed workers as migrant laborers to the United States and entertained the specialist workers. Harold thought it to be a sound business decision."

"I see." Noah said. "Ends justify means at Libertad and Cíbola, so you created a sick, symbiotic relationship. The search for gold is paramount, such an imperial attitude. I recognize this as a Catalan trait."

Jorge flashed Noah a fierce glare. "You are reminded that I am no longer shackled to Roadways, escaping the necessity for servile ways. The Catalan outlook is imperial for bona fide reasons. We enjoyed the civilizing influence of the Romans before the birth of the Christ Child, while Anglo-Saxons wandered about in the northern forests wearing hairy hides on their backs and baying at the moon." He warmed to his subject. "Charlemagne the Great freed us from the Saccrens in the eighth century while your ancestors were puzzling over Roman ruins on the sorry little island of Britain they were permitted to occupy."

Noah was ashamed for maintaining an authoritarian attitude with a man who was trying to assist him in a time of need. "Forgive me for my imperial manners. My brief stint as Ludie's groom-to-be messed with my mind. I've no desire or talent to be a big shot. Please accept my apologies."

"Apologies accepted gladly because I appreciate the situation you are in. I married a once-beautiful woman with means and learned to regret it deeply. You are actually very fortunate to be divorced from the Roadways Company, for they are intent on pursuing a road construction strategy in Mexico that may prove to be disastrous to them."

"Are they going to lose a lot of money?" Noah asked, hoping for bad news.

"On the contrary, the short-term financial gains for 'Anglo-Saxons', as I call all United States big business people, will be considerable, but the long-term risks are great, particularly if roads are built throughout Latin America."

"What are the risks in those successes? Roadways into underdeveloped regions will be a terrific thing for poor people."

"Yes, of course," Jorge said, "but as a Catalan I take an historic viewpoint. Consider, Noah, that roads can be traveled in two directions. Anglo-Saxons are at risk of being eventually overwhelmed by the Hispanics who were in the Americas a century before your ancestors. Could it be that the battle for North America may yet be won by Hispanics?"

"Not possible," Noah said. "Everything is rigged against Hispanics in this hemisphere. The United States and Canada have too much money and technology, as well as an overwhelming advantage militarily, to be conquered in a future foreseeable to me. I see increasing populations and increasing misery in Mexico and elsewhere in Latin America."

"Perhaps your vision is restricted by your distaste for assertive leadership methods. Those wishing to create crises of their own design for their ultimate benefit will think differently. There will be war between Hispanic and the so-called Anglo-Saxon cultures because of natural resources."

"Make your case," Noah said. "And show me how the Hispanics can win."

"Please observe, Noah, that the United States is a greedy consumer of natural resources, having five percent of the world's population and now using more than twenty-five percent of its natural resources. Already, you use your military to assure access to foreign oil fields for your gas-guzzling automobiles, such as the Intimidator. In the not distant future, Latin America will be invaded by the Anglo-Saxons for its natural resources. I assure you of this certain future event."

Noah could offer no immediate contradictions, reflecting that Jorge's credentials as a mining engineer in constant search for bigger and better precious metal deposits gave credence to his arguments. Noah saw that his meager efforts to provide bilingual language skills to destitute Hispanics desperate to survive was without effective purpose. He was a fraud, a trickster, leading others to believe that his abiding passion was to serve the downtrodden. But he really wanted to prove himself worthy by doing something that was so additive and distinctive that kudos would be accorded him. Why else had he built his school in the middle of the Chiapas political hotbed, and then pushed his special agenda until he drew the wrath of the beleaguered Federales? As Josiah would say, he was a nit on a gnat's ass. He tossed the maps on the truck's floor in disgust.

"Do not despair, Noah," Jorge said. "All is not lost for Hispanics, because we have already commenced our invasion of the United States and Canada using our strongest forces, rapidly increasing populations with desperate needs for water, food and shelter. Our shabby troops are penetrating the United States border in increasing numbers, relying on the goodwill of the unsuspecting fat-cats playing with the stock markets and their technical toys. They are willing to allow some of their scraps to fall from sumptuous tables in return for the Hispanics performing menial labor that is unacceptable to them."

"Hispanics will be the losers if that's their invasion," Noah said. "When economic times worsen, the border will be closed by the Migras – the United States Border Patrol – and all illegals will be forced out." As far as he was concerned, the Migras were the flip-side of the Federales.

"Time only will tell, but for now Hispanics have no other choice. We must invade now instead of waiting for the certain use of the United States military to confiscate Latin America's natural resources to sustain greedy lifestyles. Only a large, educated, politically active Hispanic population in the United States can prevent your politicians from promising and producing this invasion."

"How much time will your invasion require?"

"Two more generations, perhaps less now that NAFTA has been introduced to the power balance. United States power brokers adopted this so-called free trade initiative believing that it would further enrich them by the use of low cost labor in new factories in Mexico. This will prove to be a fatal tactic, because Hispanics will usurp the technology and know-how placed within their borders and become competitors for the very businesses the Anglo-Saxons consider their private domain."

Jorge returned to the business at hand. "But for now we have good luck, for that is Libertad behind us." He switched the truck's lights to full. "This is the route through the great rift's sand traps taken by Libertad's clients hoping for jobs in the United States. It ends in wild terrain on the Arizona border that can't be traversed by most vehicles. It is a pity that we would have been marked men in your Intimidator. Those desperate for jobs walk the border crossing. So do the human mules with drugs." He turned on a tiny dashboard light and directed it on the map in Noah's lap. "Guide us to Pendejos Punto by daylight. The path to the north beyond that place is very treacherous according to those at Libertad, but our fortune lies in that direction."

Noah scowled at the maps. "I'm on it. We're heading east by northeast." He refolded a map with care. "Tomas told me the Pendejos Punto story."

"I love to hear it because Spaniards always get their cojónes crushed." Jorge placed the gun back in the basket, swerving to avoid a sand-covered rock. "The overhead spotlights go on now. We must keep moving and stay alert, so we are not captured by those traveling this route for illegal purposes."

Noah organized his new workspace, settling in for the long night. He then checked the dashboard compass and frequently pointed out obstacles. Such teamwork made their steady progress possible. He allowed a part of his mind to reflect on Josiah's crises intervention model, concentrating on his present personal crisis. The "what is" was that he was now embarked on a risky venture – possibly a wild goose chase – because he had been all too readily reeled in by Ludie. He was a greedy Anglo seeking the easy means to pursue his own unique path, no better than all others seeking to get rich quick at Cíbola.

He stirred in his seat at the realization of this brutal truth, reluctantly examining the "could be's" available to him. The option of returning to Cíbola and completing the assignment to Ludie's satisfaction was discarded, as was the possibility of appealing to Sarah for one last financial boost enabling him to establish a new bilingual school somewhere in Latin America. Pursuing his current path with Jorge was appealing, but not without guilt for participating in yet another Cíbola-like, get-rich-quick scheme.

Deep down Noah knew that none of the "could be's" served his true "should be" which was to return to his own maverick path as a teacher of the dispossessed poor, disdaining anyone's financial support. Devoting himself to a calling that few coveted offered his best chance to avoid direct conflict with those ever eager to accumulate more property. But would he get a second chance to do it right, and for the right reasons?

Noah asked Jorge to stop for a pee break. He took on more water but was too hyped to eat the food they had aboard. Evidently, Jorge felt the same. They were now in the heart of the despoblado. With the truck's lights shut-off on this moonless night, the cold stare of the stars was intense, seeming to start at his shoulders. The ever-present westerly winds created furtive sounds in the darkness. Or was it the wind? He decided it was too cold and hurriedly got into the truck.

Jorge requested that Noah change places at four o'clock. Within fifteen minutes, they found this didn't work. Jorge needed Noah's navigational expertise and his own knowledge of the truck's capabilities to reach Pendejos Punto by daybreak.

Morning sunshine presented Pendejos Punto in its entire false splendor. Heavy concentrations of pyrite, fools gold, set aglitter a sizable section of the opposing cliffs. As he had found the case with most highly anticipated destinations, Noah found Pendejos Punto to be a disappointment. Aside from the faint but certain signs of vehicle tracks, the up-close reality was no sparkle, human refuse, and attempts at graffiti. The pyrite-infested boulders protruded out into the sands in a curving claw. At the claw's point was a stack of jagged stones from a bygone prospector's pick. Standing atop the pile was a black-hooded figure in strange garb, holding a chunk of pyrite in its right hand. Noah recog-

nized a Papago trickster's costume worn by self-appointed males intent
on creating outrageous mischief and violating tribal customs to remind
all of the ambiguities and paradoxes in their lives. How appropriate, he
thought, for his own situation.

The truck's bumper stopped less than a hand-span from the pyrite
pile. The trickster extended the hand holding the pyrite towards the
truck and stretched a leg behind it. The leg was then lowered, allowing
the trickster to bow from the waist, teetering atop the pyrite pile.

As Jorge reached for his gun, a small man with a black patch over his
right eye placed the barrel of a large pistol into his ear through the open
window. "Atencíon, gold wagon guards, you'll now vacate this vehicle.
First, the Anglo will exit and stand near my man, the trickster fool atop
the fool's gold. I'll then step down and allow this Catalan called Jorge
to join the Anglo. Jorge, you're to remain absolutely silent."

The hooded man jumped from the pyrite pile, leaped to the top of a
boulder, and seated himself. Hood wore a black priest's robe and black
sneakers. A leather vest covered with little bells and metal gewgaws
completed his costume.

"You have made a mistake," Jorge said.

Patch slammed a bullet between Jorge's legs, striking the pyrite pile.
"Atencíon, this isn't a debate. I'm a bandito holding up the stagecoach
carrying the gold stolen from Cíbola. Of this I'm certain. You two vol-
unteers are to unload quickly your ill-gotten gains."

To Noah's dismay, sixteen heavy sacks were discovered under the tar-
paulin. The top only of each sack had what Patch declared to be bona fide
raw-gold nuggets. Below this facade in each sack were pieces of worthless rock and metal bits. Jorge seemed to be equally non-plussed. Hood
approached and squatted on the ground nearby.

Patch aimed the pistol with both hands and shot Jorge in the left foot,
who fell to the ground with a loud guttural scream. "What trickery is
this Catalan? Where's the rest of my gold?" He waited for Jorge to con-

trol his pain.

Noah's mind raced with such questions as, "How did Jorge steal the gold?" and "Where's the rest of the real thing?"

Patch was intent on securing answers to these questions, and many more. He pointed the gun at Jorge's head, hammer cocked. "Tell me of the gold, Catalan. Say it true the first time, and it may benefit you. Give me grief, and I shoot you right now. No use to lie, because you revealed much to Conchita the whore last Saturday night while imbibing in my truth tonic."

Jorge fought back his pain. "Each day I would go to the melting unit with my scales in a knapsack and return with select pieces of raw gold nuggets. Always the same amount."

"What allowed this to go unquestioned for three years?" Patch asked.

"There were no other people with experience or knowledge to oppose me. I had the wisdom to remove small amounts routinely before opportunity for consolidation into gold bars. It was a beautiful plan."

"Then who made all sixteen sacks become contaminated with a like weight of useless materials of similar bulk? This, too, was a beautiful plan."

"I placed the true gold in the powder bunker below the Great Corúa," Jorge said. "Surely Emilio, the powder man, discovered it when transferring powder from lower bunkers. He has made this mischief."

"Too bad for Emilio now," Patch said. "But, for now, you and I have accounts to settle." He beckoned to Hood who leaped to his feet and pointed for Noah to go south into the despoblado. As Noah started walking, Hood kicked him in the butt. Noah trotted, and then ran as fast as he could, but every so often Hood managed to kick him in the behind again. When two shots rang out behind them, Noah ran faster, so did the hooded trickster.

Noah found himself wondering what crisis contingency plan Josiah would have in place for this event. Then he realized that Josiah would never follow Jorge into the despoblado to be his cover for a major gold theft. His what is-could be-should be process would nix this journey before it started. Noah's own plan was confined to running blindly into the despoblado as long as he could, expecting a bullet to slam into his back at any moment. He spied an outcrop of pyrite protruding out into the sand. As he dodged behind the fool's gold, he tripped on a flapping red shoelace from one of his lucky blue shoes, tumbling head-over-heels three times. From his topsy-turvy position, Noah saw the trickster doing cartwheels around him and chortling in apparent glee.

Because of his fascination with Oidak in his early years, Noah had informed himself about the role of tricksters in many cultures. They supposedly appeared in societies in crisis whose rules no longer served the needs of the people. Such mythical figures as Hermes and Loki were considered by the Greeks and Norsemen to be rebellious, god-like figures capable of bringing about fundamental change for mere mortals. Coyote and Raven served this purpose in North America.

Whose crisis is this trickster intervening in? Noah thought. Certainly not his, out in this terrible despoblado where he must be considered by all as the Anglo Prince of the Pendejos. Noah clenched closed his eyes in exhaustion and resignation. Tricksters were his patron saints. No one or nothing else wrung any piety from him, so let this sappy savior do his worst.

# Part 2
# Zipizape

# Chapter 6

Roland Zain, Ludie's knight errant, prowled about Ludie's office as he awaited her arrival. When she escorted him to the office, the big redheaded woman called Patience told him that Ludie would join him shortly. Too bad, Roland thought, that the other security agent, Derek, had been the one to pat him down for weapons, because women carrying a large caliber pistol under their jacket were very fascinating indeed. Roland's nine-shot pistol had nestled against the small of his back under his suit jacket. Derek now held it in his possession.

Patience seemed to approve of his sincere black suit, conservative necktie, and highly-polished black wingtip shoes. He explained the pronunciation and meaning of his name offered each time he invaded Anglo-Saxon lands. A zain is a large, black warhorse and is not to be spoken as rain with a z, Roland informed her, but as one would say the name Zaughn, or close enough.

The huge desk in the corner of the spacious office was of particular interest to Roland. He could detect much about a person by the manner in which they decorated their workspace. The enlarged photograph of him and Ludie in Monte Carlo was positioned so Ludie could view it while seated at the desk. A small red-and-white, thirteen-star flag of the Valais Canton in Switzerland was in a matching nearby gold frame. The rest of the desk was cleared, but Roland noted that Ludie's computer was situated so she could view a lovely fishpond in a pine grove. Certainly not the waters of Champex Lac high in the Swiss Alps, but nonetheless pleasing.

Ludie burst through the office door, rushed to Roland, and gave him a most enthusiastic hug and a kiss on the lips. "Hey, handsome, it's great to see you. Thanks for coming on such short notice." She pointed to a sofa in a corner conversation area. "Let's sit over there. Coffee and croissants are on the way."

Roland was once again enchanted by Ludie's unabashed high energy. "Hello, chérie, you look splendid. I flatter myself to believe that you wore that stunning, dark gray suit to welcome me. I remember when you purchased it at the shop in Monte Carlo."

Ludie did a pirouette. "What, this old rag. It just happened to be at the top of the clothes hamper this morning." She smoothed an imagined wrinkle over her truly fine derriere. "We're just simple country folks here in little old Chapel Hill."

Roland chuckled. "I'll watch my heart now, for you've prepared me to do your bidding. Tell me more of the dilemma you are confronted with at your Cíbola gold mine."

"Josiah will give you a full account later," Ludie said. "For now, let me say that I need you to go to Cíbola today and use your particular talents on a deep water well adjoining Cíbola mesa. This well's water is the only thing of worth down there now. Eliminate the water, and the people and the TV coverage will go away."

"So I'm to blow up the well."

"It has to be done because Harold is winning the propaganda war against Roadways. We're in danger of losing our favorable position with the Mexican authorities and Emblema Compañia. Many lucrative NAFTA-driven business opportunities are at stake."

"So I'm bound for Cíbola undercover to destroy the well, and, then, return to your arms. I can do this thing, a Zain clan specialty." Roland leered at Ludie "Perhaps rehearsal of the return to your arms portion of the program is in order prior to my departure."

Ludie seated herself by Roland and placed her hand on his knee. "You're such a naughty boy. For my part, I'll restrain myself, so I can later participate in the full program. Go to Cíbola in your full force and use your considerable swagger to the utmost. Go first to the Cíbola mesa, announce that you're the new managing director, confiscate the Intimidator automobile, and then deal with the well. Please accomplish this crisis intervention assignment for me on a free-lance basis for now. Let's not tell Josiah about destroying the well, because he appears to have a sentimental attachment to Cíbola mesa. After Grethe was killed, I was supposed to fire him, but I need him a bit longer."

"But what of the young Noah, who, I understand, holds the Cíbola managing director position, and, it appears, your hand?"

Ludie patted Roland's knee. "Noah is a very fine young man, but not suited for either position. He was informed of this yesterday and won't be present at Cíbola. It appears that he's joined Jorge Catalano's expedition to search for a new gold deposit as a boost to his ego. Will you do this thing for me, Sir Roland?"

"Your wishes are my commands, of course, but what of the priggish Harold? Isn't he loitering about?"

"Harold has been terminated from the mining group director position given him by Grethe. Josiah has, for the time being, been given these responsibilities. Would you please now go to discuss Cíbola and the mining group with him?"

Ludie escorted Roland to her office door. "By the way, the priggish Harold may also be bound for Cíbola to see if he can salvage his sagging reputation and bank account."

"And what am I to do with him?"

"You can blow his backsides off for all I care." Ludie's lips smiled, but her steel-gray eyes did not.

* * *

Roland found himself again waiting in a workspace. Josiah's situation room had much in common with a war-readiness room he had once been privileged to enter in the Swiss Army's massive bunkers under his home village of Chapex Lac. His father, Barthleme, had done much of the demolition work on this fortress masterpiece. Roland studied the large, flattened world map with a dozen black markers dotting Canada, Mexico, and the United States. His eyes searched for signs of the many road construction projects and detected many pinpricks in the map. Was Josiah defending his turf by concealing it? He made particular note of one such project in Taiwan where he had most recently been profitably employed under the sponsorship of Ludie.

Josiah entered the room and saw Roland examining his world map. "Take a good look at those mining locations, Roland. Ludie hasn't discussed your assignment with me, but I can only hope that she intends to assign the mining group to you. Have a seat, and I'll get right at the briefing."

Roland noted that Josiah's voice had all its full vigor, but he was no longer the imposing physical force he was when he first met him fifteen years ago, when Roland was twenty-five years old on his first free lance assignment. "How did Harold manage the mining group along with his Mason Company responsibilities?"

"No problem for him, because he brought his three sons into his business. Ludie calls them Harry, Larry, and Moe. Harold invested a lot of money, time, and effort in courting Ludie through Grethe. With NAFTA in play, he figured this was the best way to expand outside of Canada. You know, conquer the North American road construction business down to Panama. Being a mason, he has grand designs to be a major mover-and-shaker again."

Roland studied the black markers. "Grethe's strategy was brilliant, yes? There is great synergism between road construction and open pit mining. Did you approve of this strategy?"

"I helped Grethe invent it at Cíbola. At first, I was angry at having my career sidetracked, but Cíbola was the best assignment I ever had during my marriage. Everything you would ever want, in terms of family and work, was available on top of that beautiful mesa. But I was eager for promotion, too dumb as a thirty-five year old hotshot to know that I couldn't balance family and work by dint of effort alone."

"I understand that managers were in short supply at that time, so you were undoubtedly caught in the go-up-or-get-out phenomena. Besides, I know how exciting it is to work in a climate of crisis. The stakes are immediate and intensive, and personal wins or losses clear-cut. But be mindful of this, Josiah. If you live by the sword in the assertive crisis intervention wars, you'll most likely die by the sword, so always stay on the warhorse that brought you thus far. If you dismount, your person, as well as your character, can be assassinated by those who dare strike only when you're no longer a mounted warrior. My own father forgot this dictum and attempted to retire to a vineyard. Someone with a long memory and a long knife ended his life as he lazed in the shade of an arbor with a glass of fine wine. I'm sworn not to repeat his mistake."

The business briefing Josiah provided Roland was professional and complete, but not once did he mention Noah and his failed relationship with Ludie. In Roland's estimation, Josiah was undoubtedly disappointed that he was unable to promote Noah as his successor and eventual leader of Roadways, a most subtle bride-capture strategy. But would he tolerate a fellow mercenary – the true name for a crisis intervention specialist – such as himself at the helm of Roadways?

"It isn't like you to push those black mining markers off your platter," Roland said. "You've always sought greater responsibilities. You're not sending me on a fool's errand, are you?"

Josiah's face reddened, and he then relaxed and smiled. "Good for you, Roland. Once, I would've asked the same question. Ludie believes the mining group has outstanding potential. I'm only trying to ease myself out of Roadways in a way that's good for me and good for her." He massaged the back of his neck. "Wouldn't it be great if Sarah and I could come together someplace with Noah and support him in his work? I'll tell you what, Roland, I would get off my horse to do this, damn the consequences."

Roland wished to reward such uncharacteristic candidness. "But Noah is a mature man who has been independent of you for several years. Haven't you long since discharged your parental duties to him?"

"Obviously so, but I won't excuse myself from trying to protect him from serious harm. I can't tolerate thoughts of losing him, particularly if it's within my particular powers to shield him. Your father was in crisis intervention work. When did he cut you loose completely?"

Roland laughed ruefully. "My father, and a long line of Zains, were mercenaries. The Zains have long surrendered their personal integrity for assured rewards. I was the middle child of seven sons, perfectly positioned to be ignored. I didn't benefit from primogeniture or suffer the stresses of a second son. I envy Noah the problem you present to him"

"How can I convince him of his good fortune?"

"That's a conundrum beyond my experience or understanding, but please answer me this question. Do you wish him to grant you the unconditional love you shared when he was a child, or do you wish his survival. They may be mutually exclusive."

Josiah didn't hesitate. "His survival comes first."

"So you've made the choice and now must live with the consequences." Roland paused to reflect. "You've long been my very kind sponsor, so I say this to you with difficulty. You don't come to the work of a crisis intervention specialist naturally. Your ancestors always managed the affairs of their overlords. Your bloodline ill prepared you for the deeds you've accomplished for Roadways by dint of courage, extraordinary effort, and luck."

"You're saying that I've risen above my level of competency?" Josiah paused. "I'm not buying that, Roland, because many warriors advance from the ranks of the followers. Once a warrior, aren't you always a warrior?"

"Please consider this, Josiah." Roland, a most private person, regretted engaging in an exchange of personal confidences, but he decided to stay the course. "What I do by the accident of my birth, and long training and practice, is to employ my gifts of assertive foresight. I possess the capabilities to chose the most promising course of action with boldness and determination, ever ready for conflict."

Josiah gave Roland his rapt attention, spurring him on.

"The attitude required for constant assertive foresight is created by altitude, because height inevitably increases the depth and breadth of vision. Swiss mercenaries were once high-mountain people who became the first free men in all Europe because they could detect and counteract those attacking them from the flatlands."

Roland lubricated his throat with cold coffee. "When the Zains descended from their combes – the little, protected valleys high in the Alps – they wisely chose to mount large, black war horses – zains - providing them advantageous overviews of battlefields while in the flatlands. Zains are taught to never dismount from their horses for any reason."

"Maybe we're both out of fashion now," Josiah said. "Corporate crisis intervention could be a relic of the twentieth century."

"On the contrary, the practice of rising above a fray, identifying crucial elements, and controlling critical events will continue to thrive, because managements will no longer try to stifle crisis, but, instead, embrace them as instruments of rapid, significant change. When all is tranquil within an organization, workers at all levels are loath to change for fear of losing hard-fought-for positions and privileges. They protect their job boundaries. But chaos distracts them nicely, allowing a skilled crisis intervention specialist to implement major organization redesigns. For instance, when in Taiwan, I learned from a fellow practitioner that the Chinese character for crisis means a dangerous opportunity. So, you see, your generation rushed in to restore too quickly the prevailing order."

"What's wrong with that method?" Josiah demanded. "It's always best to get things back on track. If something's not broke, don't fix it."

"The wrong is that the rate of change has increased tremendously. To keep pace with changes outside an organization, internal changes must be even more rapid. A climate of rapid, continuous change and improvements will mark all future successful companies."

"So while the troops are scurrying about, you rearrange the furniture." Josiah appeared to be amused. "The heck with restoring order."

"No, Josiah, don't rearrange the furniture. Make it disappear, perhaps the entire building. The greater the changes desired, the greater the chaos required."

"Grethe would accept such a cold-blooded approach if the price were right, but Ludie's not cut out for the real rough stuff."

Roland was now amused. "You've much to learn about your new boss. She's far more capable than you give her credit for. What Ludie permits you to see isn't what you'll get from her. She, like myself, is a product of a clan that thrives on crises, only our methods differ."

"You're mistaken, Roland. Grethe was as tough as nails, but Ludie's amazingly decent for someone with her upbringing. She's been a little testy lately because of the business problems piling up on her."

"Your deductions are too simplistic. Ludie's, in fact, an artful dissembler."

Josiah furrowed his brow. "Please enlighten me. Is it a fatal condition?"

"Certainly not for her. I'm merely saying that she's gifted at disguising her true feelings and intentions, making it difficult to detect her true attitudes or qualities."

"But you're exempt. Right?"

"Not at all." Roland smiled. "I receive added attentions. But, for me, this makes our romantic jousting even more exciting. My assertive foresight skills will eventually win our courtship tournament."

Josiah studied Roland. "Are you now declaring yourself to be Roadways' chief crisis intervention specialist because your kind sponsor is on his way out?"

"Not me. I'll limit my specialty to producing focused chaos on demand until instructed otherwise. My father did instruct me to never make an enemy of a fellow horseman unless absolutely necessary."

Roland departed from the situation room, leaving Josiah, hands clasped before him, at the table. As he waited to say his goodbyes to Ludie in a reception area outside her office, Patience continued to monitor his movements. Her intense blue eyes missed nothing, nor did they show any warmth when he glanced at her. For Roland, this was an attractive feature in a woman, but in his estimation Ludie's steely-gray gaze was far more dangerous, his kind of woman for his bride-to-be. But assertiveness alone wouldn't capture Ludie. A modicum of cunning would also be required, which, surely, would be appreciated by her in due course.

As Roland left the Roadways corporate compound with his gun back in his possession, he was again reminded of the false security Ludie had provided herself with the two security guards. They would be but a nuisance if anyone of a serious terrorist persuasion wished to punish Roadways for their misdeeds, imagined or real. And the pleasant town of Chapel Hill offered no protection of consequence. Although no less than twenty so-called protestors were assembled, no uniformed police were evident. How was one to know that all in attendance were only the pampered children of affluent parents?

Roland drove slowly throughout Chapel Hill's orderly, tree-lined streets in ever-widening circles around the Roadways headquarters building. He encountered only seemingly content, industrious people going about their separate businesses. Since it was a university town, there were a great number of attractive young people. Roland mused that good economic times were certainly reflected in the well-being of those benefiting fully in the bounty afforded.

But what if this was snatched away from them, he thought? What could or would be the attitudes of these youths toward a corporate entity such as Roadways. Certainly events in the nineteen sixties and seventies in the United States could provide some answers without straining the imagination. He had witnessed massive disruptions in other so-called stable countries.

Warming to his subject as he drove his rental car to the airport, Roland considered how the flatlands of North Carolina offered no natural protection whatsoever from invading forces, particularly from the south. This central state area was called the Piedmont, as if it were lying at the base of mountains. Mountains? The highest point in the entire state was but six thousand feet. Not one of these hills rose above a timberline.

By the time he reached the airport, Roland happily decided that the new Roadways headquarters would be relocated to the Valais Canton in Switzerland. He could envision the perfect site. The formidable granite building would hug an outcrop high on Mont La Breya overlooking Lac de Champex and the Swiss national alpine research gardens. He and Ludie would build a personal residence at timberline, well above the headquarters building, to occupy in the complete security and serenity availably only in a small valley atop a high mountain.

# Chapter 7

Francisco Vasquez didn't share the slow pace of Saturday morning at Libertad Most workers rested from their frenzied Friday night duties, but he would use his day to assess damage, resupply, and protect his turf. He completed his daily run in the desert and walked into Libertad's back gate. No pain, no gain, Francisco thought. He was going to stay in the one hundred and sixty-seven pound class this time. He would cool down in his sweats by making a quick check of all Libertad departments, and then go to his shop to make more of the simple solar stoves that were selling well to migrants and locals.

As he entered the zipizape dance area, Francisco spoke in Spanish to several female attendants. All looked tired because Magdalena, the featured dancer, had again succeeded in making the Friday night attraction a raucous free-for-all. After a couple of years in the Sonora, Francisco still thought in English. His Spanish-speaking skills were rusty when he arrived, thanks to his Shoshone mother, Sego Lily, and schooling in English only through four years of college in Idaho. His Papago father, Pedro, born on the Arizona Papago reservation, never valued his native language or Spanish.

"Hola, Juan, how does it go?" Francisco didn't linger to chat with the chief cook for the eating area. Another class of migrant job seekers would graduate today and start their northern trek across the despoblado, the awful, deadly deserted wilderness to the United States and jobs tomorrow. Yeah, sure, lots and lots of great jobs, Francisco mused. And the poor desperate bastards would be at the mercy of their paid guides called coyotes for good reasons. These greedy tricksters promised migrants safe passage across the despoblado for outrageous fees and, once paid, often abandoned them, proving yet again that coyotes of any stripe aren't to be trusted.

Francisco recalled that he grew up on the Fort Hall Indian Reservation near Pocatello on a steady diet of folk tales about Old Man Coyote, the great Shoshone tribal trickster capable of playful pranks, roguish sexual romps, or savagely destructive deceptions. Because his brother, Roberto, his senior by three years, was Pedro's constant companion working on the family hog farm, Francisco was relegated to working with Sego Lily in a big converted horse barn, making beaded buckskin clothing for the Fort Hall trading post. Discovering that he wasn't a gifted maker of moccasins, Francisco became the repair guy for the clothing business, and eventually for most of the reservation.

He became increasingly financially self-sufficient as a fix-it whiz for sports equipment – fishing reels a specialty because as a five-year old he dismantled reels instead of alarm clocks. This eventually led to his getting a regular sportsmen clientele who convinced him that the ways of the white people must be superior. On weekends, these fat-cats drove up to the Vasquez shack in shiny cars and pickups on their way to and from trout fishing or goose hunting on the American Falls reservoir. Francisco's prison was the white man's playpen.

Sego Lily's clothing-maker female companions respected her story-telling skills because she learned this craft from her grandfather, Singing Owl, a medicine man renowned for his Old Man Coyote epic tales sung during annual sacred Sun Dances that were held on the reservation during each summer solstice. Evidently, Francisco puzzled out, Old Man Coyote was credited with the origins of the Shoshone people.

He lived in a mythical past when animals had the power of speech and set the customs the Shoshone later followed.

Francisco was fascinated by Old Man Coyote's trickster exploits, but, in his estimation, he was a loose cannon careening about the Great Basin despoblado, including Idaho, Nevada, and Utah, doing more harm than good. The prescriptions for survival before the white people arrived were no longer potent, so none were available for their current crisis. The coyote trickster was largely responsible for the Shoshone people being penned up on a reservation by the white people – so much for religious nostrums. But the Old Man Coyote tales also included descriptions of explicit sexual activities told to young Francisco by the women with glee, so sex education was included in his indoctrination into the Shoshone's notions of cosmology.

Reflections on his early exposure to the Shoshone half of his religious roots were pushed aside as Francisco viewed the decaying Catholic chapel in the shrine site's center. Before the spring dried up, Papago Folk Catholicism thrived here. As explained by Ojo Solo, this movement was a form of native Christianity built from elements taken from Hispanic and Papago religious concepts and practices, and combined in unique ways. Catholic ritual behavior was integrated into the Papago system for preserving health and balance in families and communities.

The old mission that the Franciscan priests had built atop the Papago shrine site three hundred years ago had never been so ill-used. Ojo Solo and his itinerant hawkers of shoddy goods, the bird catchers, moved in when the water well replaced the dried-up spring atop the mesa and renamed it Libertad. The main building was now the Chapel Cantina, where Ojo Solo's bruisers dispensed the sacred saquaro wine to prompt enthusiastic vomiting at the puking place. Francisco held his nose – hoo boy, better get the clean-up crew back over here.

Francisco passed by the sleeping sheds where the zip was put into the zape, repeatedly. Ojo Solo, who had added whore master to his resume, was now pushing to let the mafioso dope dealers in. Over my dead body, Francisco thought. We came here to pick a few pockets, not screw these poor people to death or fry their brains. No use going to the old stone baptistery at the front of the property, now the Baptistery Bank. It was locked with all receipts, be it money or barter, from the past week. Tomorrow would be profit sharing day, good old pay day. Profits were the name of Libertad's game and must be measured with care and allocated with precision by the grotesque guardian Godzilla to reduce bloodshed. After hurriedly passing through Ojo Solo's bird catcher stalls filled with tawdry sexual materials and gaudy religious icons, Francisco lingered in his own survival utensil stalls in the southwest corner of Libertad, deciding to wait here for Ojo Solo so they could discuss tactics for tonight's candidato zipizape, their biggest payday of the week. Saturday night in an old mining town was more than just a ditty at Libertad.

Lately, Francisco didn't welcome time for reflections about his own growing greed, because he was clinging to a slippery slope leading to his becoming as bad as, or worse than, Ojo Solo, who couldn't help himself. Francisco was in danger of going beyond being a selfish trickster into unfettered greed and cruelty. All he really wanted to do was be a follower, making and selling quality crafts at a fair price, but his trickster habits, adopted as protective cover, were sucking him into being a major participant in the evil entity called Libertad. Ambivalence pushed Francisco more frequently into his trickster mode. He had developed much of his trickster-self early in life to cope with Roberto, the uptight family heir. Early trickster training was now serving him well, too well, for his peace of mind.

Sego Lily, recognizing that the Vasquez family paradigm didn't favor Francisco, had encouraged him to leave the Fort Hall Reservation to pursue his own path. She hoped that he would join members of her Tendoy clan in the isolated Duck Valley Reservation in northern

Nevada, so she was aghast when he declared that he wanted to be like white people. Why not? They had the deck stacked in their favor, and there would be no fair deals during his lifetime.

Francisco had argued that the Shoshone people were at the very bottom of the totem pole and always would be. Five hundred years ago when white people invaded the Americas, the Papagos, at least, had constructed ingenious irrigation systems and ball courts. The Shoshone were migrant stone-age remnants subsisting largely on roots, toads, and insects. He contended that living conditions for many at Fort Hall were little better than they were for their stone-age ancestors.

So after finishing eight years of schooling on the reservation, Francisco had broken with Shoshone tradition and attended high school in nearby Pocatello instead of working on the hog farm. A religious group, calling themselves Methodists, had kindly housed and fed Francisco and enabled him to attend high school, explaining that they had been special friends to the Shoshone people for one hundred and fifty years. Eagerness to learn white people's ways had prompted him to attend Sunday church services throughout his high school years, but he had never gotten the message intended. In spite of all the promises of a perfect order in a heaven of uncertain whereabouts, and a soon-to-come Savior on earth, he had found the Christian recorded history as savage and chaotic as that described in the Shoshone folktales. Could Jesus be a failed trickster who was coming back to set things right? If so, Francisco thought that Old Man Coyote ought to be allowed to return and take another crack at redesigning the Shoshone culture.

Old Man Coyote had decreed that no Shoshone was to be a leader of the tribe, except when a war chief was required to repel attacks from enemy tribes. Francisco observed that this was also a sound doctrine for him while off reservation, because the local white people considered an assertive Indian in their midst to be an oxymoron. He had decided to be a follower, but a canny one resorting to trickster ways to assert himself covertly as needed. The wrestling ring had become his area of combat. He had made his assertiveness palatable to white people by clowning around in the ring with his weird haircut and hip-huckster patter. While the audience was enjoying belly laughs, he was body slamming and pinning opponents.

Ojo Solo wandered through the survival utensil stalls, sneering at the objects for sale to those soon to arrive as next week's migrant trainees, and illegals returning with pay checks. He took care of his own resupply, because Francisco wouldn't touch the goods he favored. There was a war raging within Libertad between Ojo Solo and Francisco, but Magdalena had them both by the cojónes, their balls locked in her hock, for sure.

As usual, Ojo Solo was hung over and surly. "Hola, Francisco the Good, you have had your little trot in the desert, no doubt dreaming of the Cíbola scrap piles. A pity you failed to make the big bribe to the young Anglo for the water while on the mesa."

Francisco knew Ojo Solo was disgusted with him because he, Francisco, didn't yet possess his thirst for depravity and bloodshed. "Now that Cíbola has stopped gold mining operations, these are dangerous times for our investments." He looked up to the top of the mesa only one mile to the south. "Jorge promised water from the well for our job security, but he nor the young Anglo can help us now. Here's hoping we have better luck with the next Anglo managing director."

In fact, Francisco did think about the Cíbola scrap piles often. There were enough materials in one-of-a-dozen scrap heaps to sustain many Mexican families for several years, once they were recycled. Recover and recycle, that's what his business in Libertad was all about, much to the scorn of Ojo Solo.

Last Tuesday while visiting Cíbola mesa, Francisco couldn't resist wandering through the maintenance building that could accommodate easily a hundred shop students. Yeah, sure, Francisco thought,

Roadways will probably end up making junk of the amazing facility and take a tax write-off, or one of those accounting loophole things. Francisco also had visited Tomas' work area, a shop teacher's dream.

Francisco flexed his fingers, because he would like to throttle Ojo Solo, the sick, ornery, little coyote. But he looked so woebegone Francisco backed off. "It's Magdalena isn't it? She's jerking your chain about going to Nevada. Give her up, she's no damn good."

"Atencíon, Francisco. She only needs to leave Libertad. What makes you so holy, the stupid hair cut?"

Francisco rubbed the shaved bald spot atop his head. The Coronado circle was suntanned from his runs in the desert. His university wrestling coach, a history professor, had dubbed him Coronado in his freshman year because of his name, Francisco Vásquez. It was a great trickster gimmick when he got the goofy haircut, helping him win two national titles. He had given up the hairstyle for Debbie when they were married after graduation and settled into the yuppie life with their teaching jobs. So he had gone nuts when he lost his job, Debbie, and his physical conditioning. The Coronado-cut had gotten him back on track to clean living and a search for Pedro's Papago roots in the Sonora. His mother's Shoshone roots in Idaho, the entire Tendoy family tree, were glad to see him go.

Ojo Solo scowled. "I buy your choir boy act until I remind myself that you've survived in the Sonora for two years. You, my junior business partner, made the bribe offers for water for survival bird catchers only, ignoring the sexual enterprise. You endangered zipizape, the big money maker."

Tired of Ojo Solo's bitching and moaning, Francisco changed the subject. "You missed candidato zipizape last Saturday night because you drank too much booze. Too bad, I was fantastic."

"You are a fool to play the fool for these losers." Ojo Solo lowered his voice. "You may now confess. You delivered Magdalena's panties to the preening Catalan, didn't you?"

"Get off that stuff, Ojo Solo. You know I never do that for Her Highness. I've told you that Jorge barfed all over himself before he left the Chapel Cantina, but he didn't pass interrogation. He's too well known locally to be a candidato."

"A pity, for it would be a pleasure to learn that Godzilla won an award." Ojo Solo smiled with thoughts of past mayhem. "I try to support you, so you support my need to be in Las Vegas with Magdalena as my mistress. We'll live in luxury, and she will dance her gold-digger heart out in extravagances I finance with drug money."

"Good for you and big problems for me," Francisco said. "I'm stuck in Libertad without water because you bring Guardia down on us for a drug bust."

Ojo Solo turned away, his turn to change the subject.

Francisco ground his teeth in frustration. Pedro was right about him, a gutless second son trying to get rich quick to cover past failures. Pedro had given up on him in disgust when Francisco had read about Cíbola Mesa in the newspaper, returned to his Coronado haircut, and migrated to Mexico for work. Roberto had busted a gut laughing at him and called him "wrong-way Francisco." No one gets rich quick, Pedro warned him. Slow and steady on the hog farm was the way to go.

But Pedro's career path counseling had been too little, too late as far as Francisco was concerned. He had no clear path inside his family because Roberto was accorded the higher ranking, so he had resigned himself to the pecking order. Pedro had called him a pendejo for trying to be like white people. After his failed marriage to Debbie, he had had to plead guilty as charged. Some folks do some weird things searching for loving and caring.

"Atención," Ojo Solo said. "A large black vehicle approaches the well."

Francisco stared at the low structure of concrete and high protective fencing that marked the precious well between Libertad and Cíbola.

"Well, damn, who now? Maybe Guardia's freaking out and bringing in battle equipment to be ready for your mafioso drug buddies."

The peace of Saturday disappeared as a growing group of shrine attendants and bird catchers joined Francisco and Ojo Solo in observing events at the well one-half mile away. A pair of shoddy binoculars Francisco borrowed from a bird catcher's stall revealed a dark-headed man dressed in black unlocking the security gate, making a detailed inspection of the entire automated facility, exiting, and locking the gate behind him. He was driving the magnificent black Intimidator of Francisco's dreams.

Then, in two nimble leaps, the man was standing on top of the vehicle. He noted the pipeline that carried water up to the mesa. It disappeared a few yards from the guarded well, covered to protect it from the overburden that sloughed off the mesa. Francisco knew that the pipeline was fitted into a cleft in the cliffs for its eventual destination at the two water tanks.

"Atencíon, atencíon," Ojo Solo muttered as the man turned about and looked towards Libertad.

Francisco was not certain that the man was actually scanning the hidden trench that carried water and electricity to Libertad. Francisco had penetrated the barriers and tapped into these resources without approval. This was a well-kept secret outside the Sonora. Jorge was the richer for it. The man reached the ground in a single leap, entered the Intimidator, and charged directly toward Libertad.

"Fetch Godzilla from the Baptistery Bank," Ojo Solo said.

"Try to turn him away, Ojo Solo," Francisco said. "Keep your pit bull under control."

Ojo Solo adjusted the black patch covering his right eye to gain more of his desired pirate appearance. "Yes, Francisco the Good, the olive branch first, then a bribe offer. If he has little sense and no luck, his bones are bruised. If he continues to threaten our water, perhaps we have a candidato."

When he had confiscated the abandoned shrine site, Ojo Solo had dubbed it Libertad. Hell, everyone wants freedom. Ojo Solo had managed security well in the early days, but as profits increased, so did his needless brutality, particularly against Anglos. "Poor guy", Francisco thought, "he wants revenge for the loss of his eye, even if it was his own fault". Francisco observed him at work at the entrance gate.

Ojo Solo assumed his best bird-catcher demeanor. "Good day, Your Excellency, how may the humble attendants of this sacred shrine be of service to you?"

"I wish to speak to your leader." The man, perhaps an Anglo, spoke Spanish well.

Ojo Solo offered a bird-catcher smile. "And who may that be, por favor?"

"I've no idea." The Anglo was large, handsome, and impatient. "Do it now! Mañana's too late."

The arrogant Anglo air of superiority set off Ojo Solo. "You'll go away now. You've no need of our wares, and we've no need for yours, whatever your wares may be."

The Anglo almost retreated, almost. He turned to his vehicle and then pivoted about. "I need to speak to someone about the operations of the deep well. Can you understand what I'm saying?"

"Certainly," Ojo Solo said. "You're threatening our water, our life's blood, by whatever authority you believe you have. How much money do you want, a one-time payment?"

The Anglo looked amused. "I don't want your money." He surveyed the stalls. "Given what I see here, Libertad can't afford my price. Too bad for you."

Ojo Solo was a pirate in looks only, but he often forgot. He dashed at the Anglo and took a roundhouse swing at his head. The Anglo shifted his weight and slapped Ojo Solo to the ground. He looked more surprised than Ojo Solo.

Ojo Solo rubbed his face and beckoned for Godzilla, who looked like a giant mortician in his black coveralls, seven feet of muscle, fury, and hatred. He had one ear, no nose, no hair or eyebrows, and a face so scarred no one was certain of his ethnic origins. The Anglo had the good sense to retreat, but Godzilla made a cat-like capture move and shoved the man to the ground.

"Enough, Ojo Solo, call Godzilla off while I find out the Anglo's name."

Ojo Solo gave Francisco that sick little smile of his and said nothing. Godzilla picked the man up shoulder high and slammed him down. His feet did little-steps, a sign that stomping was next.

Francisco leaped forward and kicked the big hunk in the ass to turn him around, and punched him in the nub of his nose holes to get him to charge. Godzilla obliged, and Francisco gave him his patented headlock and hip thrust. Beautiful. The big slob did a high dive and landed on his face. For a battle-scarred brawler, he had lots to learn about his job.

"Go, Bengals, go!" Francisco hollered. But a one hundred and sixty-seven pounder wasn't going to defeat Godzilla using NCAA wrestling rules; best use Libertad etiquette. Francisco chased down Ojo Solo who was leaving the field of combat, placed a hammerlock on him, and instructed him to order Godzilla to return to his kennel at the Baptistery Bank.

Francisco bent over the man. "My name is Francisco Vasquez. What's your name?"

"My name is Roland Zain, Roadways' new Cíbola managing director." Zain fainted.

Francisco was so surprised he spoke in English. "Now that takes the rag off the bush. We're goners, stupid goners. Let's patch him up and do an interrogation. He could be a candidate for Saturday night zipizape."

# Chapter 8

Two men carried Roland to a comfortable bed in a pleasant room in a low adobe building. A vision of a small Olmec goddess in a white, fluffy robe materialized at his bedside accompanied by Francisco, his savior. The goddess – she smelled wonderful – felt all his bones with practiced hands, nodded to Francisco, and made Roland swallow two capsules. Before he could ask about the Intimidator he had secured from the gate guard called Tomas earlier in the day, he was asleep.

Francisco awakened Roland at sunset. A smile further broadened his copper face, bracketed by battered ears. "How are you feeling?"

"Surprisingly well, considering that Godzilla thought I was the ball in a rugby scrum." Roland stood and flexed his neck muscles. "How did you best that big beast?"

"I got lucky," Francisco said.

"Has he been back for a return match?"

"Godzilla's a strange guy. He just follows orders – nothing personal. But never try the same move on him twice. That could be fatal. Come outside with me to test your body parts."

Roland followed Francisco through an outside door to the western exterior of Libertad. The Intimidator, newly washed, was parked in a sizable junkyard. Francisco pointed to a nearby, oversized van on massive tires. "Can we talk swap, beauty for my beast and some bucks?"

"Very tempting indeed." Roland chuckled. "But I've developed a passion for my black beauty. Has my pistol remained under the front seat?"

"It's still there, but you should pack it. Godzilla respects heavy armament."

After retrieving and examining the pistol, Roland tucked it in its familiar niche under his belt against his back. He mused that he must be entering his dotage to have left it in Intimidator. Although destroying the well promised to be a routine task for him, he must maintain all assertive crisis intervention disciplines, including doing anything that was disagreeable as soon as possible.

"You must have been really zonked," Francisco said. You haven't said a word about the dynamic Magdalena."

"I dreamt of her, but I decided that a nubile female as hot-looking as Magdalena is spoken for and very well guarded."

"That's not how it works with our Magdalena, believe you me." Francisco pointed to the door from which they exited. "Come and see the rest of my survival utensils operations. This junk yard is my raw materials warehouse."

Roland appreciated Francisco's easy air of camaraderie, kind of a fellow athlete sort of thing. Roland was past his fortieth birthday, but he kept fit as part of his personal survival plan. Francisco escorted him throughout what he called the survival half of Libertad. They ate excellent beans and cornbread at common trestle tables, observed crafts-making expertise in a first-rate blacksmith shop, and admired survival merchandise in bird catcher stalls. Roland declined to browse in the stalls on the sexual side; his libido never needed prompting.

All those encountered insisted that Roland attend what was called zipizape at ten p.m. Francisco jokingly threatened to call Godzilla if he refused. Roland washed up in a room adjoining Francisco's, the same he occupied following Godzilla's trouncing. He calculated that the work he had to do at the nearby well was best done in the wee hours of the morning, so mingling with the locals was good cover for him.

"What does zipizape mean?" Roland asked. "Everyone seems to be looking forward to it."

"It really means a rowdy dance or even a free-for-all brawl, but we've made it a Mardi Gras of sorts. O. K. , so that's the way it started. It's now a slick, sick fiesta to sell booze and broads. Worse yet, I'm part of the show."

Francisco changed into a black priest robe and a vest covered with bells, sequins, and donna religious metals. He looked like an ancient sorcerer in the dimly lit room except for his black high-top sneakers. He took a black hood from a chest drawer. "I wear this hood doing my zipizape act. It was fun at first, but I'm sick and tired of it. That prima Magdalena won't let anyone replace me, claims it will upset the integrity of the show. What a colossal pain in the ass she's become! But, hey, she's the one bringing in most of the money."

He slumped on his bed. "Lately she's even been trying to get me to deliver her panties to her stud du jour, fat chance." He examined his costume. "These are authentic trappings of a noted Papago trickster. He did the sewing and bead work. He died of a gunshot wound over in Imuris during a performance I was watching. His job was to amuse, confuse, and abuse folks, tossing in an occasional outrageous act. The Papagos need these guys now more than ever before. Tricksters are boundary-crossers who try to get folks to change their ideas on what's right or wrong. The Papagos' notions of acceptable behavior are boxing them in. It's dangerous work if you don't know your crowd, kind of like an open-air, high-wire act. I bought the costume from his widow."

"Why do you do this Francisco?"

"Money, and, for me, lots of it. Shortly after I found I couldn't work at Cíbola using my specialty, I met Ojo Solo and started doing business here. Magdalena wandered through on her way to the States, and Ojo Solo recruited her for the dancing."

"Then Magdalena is not being manipulated by Ojo Solo, or you?"

Francisco snickered and then burst into loud laughter. "That devious little dickens bamboozled us. She's a folkloric dancer lusting for a showgirl job in Las Vegas. We gave her a free hand, and she ended up ruling the roost."

"Is Ojo Solo her favorite?"

"I'm not sure the poor schmuck ever scored." Francisco enjoyed his second laugh. "Magdalena decides who and when she beds and bogs a guy. She's lusty, but fussy. I've never made the lineup as her quickie-consort."

Roland masked his excitement. "So, what's Ojo Solo's agenda? He's not a happy man?"

"He's trying to get into the drug smuggling business big time so he can be a big-shot. He could be a real player with a strategic location with water at the head of the despoblado route to Arizona. I want to move my operations a mile west of Libertad, so I tried to make a deal for separate water and electric lines with Noah, the last Cíbola managing director, but he skipped town. Could we do some business?

"No, sorry, Francisco. I make no alliances, because I'm a freelance specialist going where I wish when I wish. My work at Cíbola will be soon finished."

"Like the specialists Jorge hired at Cíbola?"

"Close enough. I come from a long line of Swiss mercenaries. The name of our game is to get paid for fighting on someone else's territory, and then go on to the next battle. I travel light and alone, always hoping that the next assignment will be the dream job that makes me independently wealthy. The older I become, the more I dream of such a job."

"You're in the right place at Cíbola, but too damn late. There's an unreality about everyone's dreams at Cíbola, including mine. It's like everything is based on getting something for nothing. Or it's more like the troubles in our lives before we arrived at Cíbola push us to do wrong things to the people living here for our selfish purposes." Francisco rubbed the tonsure circle atop his head. "Until I invented Coronado the Great Wrestler in college, I made it too easy for everyone to assign me the second-son role. You know, low-to-no expectations. Go be a jock, Francisco Vásquez, or maybe a bullfighter. Why not? Just get out of town, so you don't embarrass your father and older brother. My father probably doesn't have a drop of Spanish blood in him, but he adopted a Spanish name and their tradition that the eldest son inherits all his property. The younger son must fend for himself. The original Coronado and I do have that in common. As a second son, he had to prove his manhood by exploring for gold in the Americas."

"But your family was honoring you by naming you Francisco Vasquez. There's a fascination with the Coronado expedition's search for the seven golden cities of Cíbola in this region more than four hundred years ago."

"My father picked Francisco Vásquez from a road sign as he escaped Arizona for horse stealing. He wanted to name me Pepe, but my mother said it sounded like a Mexican cartoon character and sneaked Francisco on the birth certificate. No one used the name until I got to college. Hells bells, I invented myself."

"Don't we all?" Roland said. "The trick is to keep reinventing yourself, so you don't have to be accountable to anyone."

"Damned if I know why you worry. But look what I did to myself. I learned to wrestle real well when I discovered that the mat was a level field of competition. The raggedy-ass Indian kid could be as good as he wanted to be in a place where equal opportunity rules applied. No lie, I really kicked ass."

He sighed. "Stupid me, I got so full of myself I tried to bring my championships off the mat into the real world and got pounded back to a raggedy-ass Indian trickster for stepping over the line. And I'm dreaming to think that I can fit in down here in the Sonora. Half Papago genes don't cut it."

Francisco stood and made a leaping, complete turn. "Back to reality where the sexual team is beating the crap out of the survival team. It's getting so the attendants need the zipizape more than the clients. Go to the Chapel Cantina now and check it out. One of my guys will take you there and to your seat in the arena in time for the big show."

* * *

Ojo Solo, sporting a tuxedo and a broad smile, met Roland as he entered the Chapel Cantina. "I've held your reservation for you, Anglo." He led Roland to the only empty stool at a large circular bar. "Have a drink, and accept my apologies for allowing Godzilla to harm you. You're an honored guest tonight."

Roland eyed the tawny drink placed before him in a tall, frosted glass. "I'm a white wine drinker. This looks lethal." He must keep a clear head to destroy the well with efficiency after this little local gala.

"Not to worry, for that is a touch only of the sacred saguaro wine for you. Francisco explained that you were able to best me because you're a professional killer, something like a ninja guy."

Roland saluted Ojo Solo and drained half the glass, delicious, really refreshing. He looked about the crowded, noisy cantina with renewed interest. The interior of the old church was lit by tiny, twinkling lights draped over the altar and several religious figures in wall recessions. Ten burly attendants dressed in white manned the inner space of the circular bar, dispensing libations from several refrigerated units.

"You like the Magdalena Special, Anglo?"

"Excellent." Roland drained the glass. "No, gracias, not another."

Ojo Solo seated himself beside Roland on a stool that miraculously become vacant. Two fresh drinks appeared. Eurhythmic music insinuated itself into the chapel, featuring drums, sticks, rattles, and a string instrument. The mounting excitement inside the boisterous shrine was palpable. Reeling men constantly beat a retreat to a door at the back of the building amid shouts of congratulations and thanks.

The historic place prompted Roland to improve Ojo Solo's knowledge of his own history, after lubricating his throat with a sip, or two, of the local wine. "I'm not an Anglo, Ojo Solo, but a Francés. My ancestors can be traced back to the tenth century in the Swiss Alps."

"I'm from the great shrine site of the Sonora, Magdalena de Kino, so my name is Kino," Ojo Solo said. "My mother gave me to the Catholics, so they could make a priest of me. I taught them a few lessons and departed. Even the devil was an angel when he began."

Ojo Solo lifted his eye patch to reveal an ugly, empty socket. "It must be so tranquil to live on a mountain or a mesa, so no one mutilates or plunders you. Someday, I will live in such a high place in Nevada. I'll take my God, gold, with me. Gold must be your God, too Francés, or you wouldn't be in Libertad."

"Much gold is good to hoard on a high mountain, but once there, it's no longer the deity. Nothing is supreme to the mountain itself."

"Atencíon, Francés, that was well said." Ojo Solo tipped his glass to Roland. "Too bad that you're but a passing pilgrim. We could again debate your foolish notion that rocky heights can replace gold."

"So you occupied Libertad when it was a dried-up shrine site, and Francisco brought you water and electricity. Your own pilgrimage brought you to the right place at the right time."

"Francisco the Good did little of importance. He's but a handyman. I changed the name to Libertad. He thought it meant to enable free-born men to gain freedom from poverty by preparing them for jobs in El

Norte." Ojo Solo drained his oversized glass. "Libertad means to be free in this place to do whatever you please. That's what the priests did when they took this shrine from the Papagos."

A small man in ragged clothes reeled into Ojo Solo's stool. Roland took the opportunity to quaff another of the harmless drinks placed before him.

Directing the man toward the back door, Ojo Solo patted him on the back. "You're a good man when you're drunk." He took a generous slug of his drink. "It's the duty of a Papago man to drink the sacred saguaro wine until dizzy and puke on the ground. It brings the rains."

"Did the Franciscan priests teach this doctrine?" Roland asked.

Ojo Solo laughed loudly and slapped the bar. "They retreated long ago. I use Papago ancient ways and some of their nonsense to make this a site for men to do what they please."

"What role do the women play?"

Ojo Solo jabbed his right forefinger repeatedly into his circled left thumb and forefinger. "They are play things only. Magdalena has yet to learn this, but I'm an entrepreneur first. At Libertad we are all men of the salt. A Papago man doesn't have his cojónes until he has walked the despoblado and brought back the salt. Men once journeyed to salt deposits at the Gulf of California, but now we send them to El Norte to earn their salt." He stood and straightened his tuxedo. "I'm a good man, and I'm drunk. I go to the puking place and prove my manhood. You've yet to do this deed, Francés."

Roland thought Ojo Solo's performance was well done, a good host for a collection of clueless, mongrel flatlanders who were about to lose their precious well. Ojo Solo was proof that in a country of blind men the one-eyed man is king. The same silent man led him to the zipizape arena, seated him, and departed. More than a hundred men crowded the sandy, open-air, walled space. A large stage raised several feet above the sand was before them. After the chaos and stench in the Chapel

Cantina, the low murmurs of the men under the low-hanging stars were hypnotic. Roland occupied a plush red chair, front and center; all others were seated on rough benches.

He accepted with thanks another of the refreshing drinks delivered on a silver tray by the burly attendant who had served him in the cantina. If Ludie could see me now, Roland thought, she could admire my capabilities to prosper out in the crazy, cruel world of people scuffling to survive. He, Roland Zain, would be a great president of the Roadways Company, a true leader of men. Would it be beyond reason to anticipate that he would be given a bachelor party with the enticing Magdalena? Certainly not, for he was already being accorded the courtesy of an honored guest.

Roland heard murmurs of "Candidato, Candidato, Candidato" all about him before enough light to tax the Sonora electrical grid struck the audience in the face. Then multiple speakers, blaring the same music suggested in the cantina, riveted them to their seats for the moment. Twelve women in scant, sequined costumes walked sedately onto center stage. They were Indian, shapely, and of equal medium height. As soon as they bowed to the audience in graceful unison, zip-izape struck the arena.

The production seemed to emulate the debauch the men undertook in the Chapel Cantina and puking place. Leaping female bodies and the music portrayed ultimate success by virtue of the descent to earth of the rain god to saturate the sands and nourish the gardens. Respectful silence reigned in the audience. Roland sipped a drink and made an adjustment to his pistol's positioning to increase his comfort in the plush red chair.

"Coronado, Coronado, Coronado." Many in the audience knew the program. The masked figure in the flowing robe and clown trappings charged through the laughing men and catapulted himself upon the stage via a well-positioned trampoline. He fondled the buttocks of a nearby dancer and clutched his crotch. Delighted catcalls resounded. The trickster then reentered the audience, lifted his robe, and took a generous piss on the head of a comatose celebrant slumped on a bench. Denunciations and threats were called out. A medley of outrages followed, featuring bodily-function humor and sexual perversions, designed to ridicule priests, shamans, and all believers. After a finale featuring the sexual harassment of each of the twelve females, the trickster swept by Roland with a high five and disappeared from the arena. Roland quelled a moment of urgent queasiness with a drink. A man of his pending stature couldn't frequent the puking place, no way.

"Godzilla, Godzilla, Godzilla," demanded the men.

The next production brought Godzilla on stage as the Great Corúa. The not-subtle message was that without the sacred serpents to guard Papago springs, there was no water, and therefore no life for humans. Roland watched the glistening bodies of the twelve Corúa maidens and deduced that the huge feathered serpent Godzilla represented didn't cause an effect for humans. Evidently, it existed for its own cosmic purposes, raw Mother Nature at her work.

"Magdalena, Magdalena, Magdalena." The men's chant was fervent but reverent.

Roland participated in the third production for several reasons. It was an explicit depiction of a fertility rite, the twelve temple whores wore no underpants, and the magnificent Magdalena starred, wearing scant panties. He had a sane moment when he could assess that the entire performance was truly well done, of high professional quality. Then Magdalena's magic robbed him of his rational thoughts. Her performance style was an amalgamation of gypsy flamenco, Tina Turner, and Mary Lou Retton. The eurhythmics she could achieve with her Venus-like, five-foot body excited the men to frenzy. The supporting casts' frequent split-leg cartwheels were in perfect counterpoint.

"Ole! ole!, ole!" Roland was standing and shouting in unison with the other men as Magdalena ended the show with a spectacular leaping split in the center of the similarly positioned twelve. Roland, choking back an urge to vomit, hurled his long-empty glass against the stage, and joined the ranks of the standing men.

"Candidato, Candidato, Candidato," roared the men.

Magdalena walked to the front of the stage as lights flooded the seating area. She seemed to look into the hungry eyes of each man. Slowly, she removed her panties and directed two burly attendants to deliver them to Roland.

Roland saw the panties depart from the stage, but the numbness that started in his face overcame his entire body, and he slumped back into his seat. The chosen consort of the vestal virgin was unable to rise to the occasion. The two attendants lifted Roland in the red chair and slowly carried him from the arena to the incantations of the men.

"Magdalena, no, no."

"Godzilla, sí, sí."

"Magdalena, no, no."

"Godzilla, sí, sí."

* * *

Roland was awakened in the adobe house by the sensation of many boulders trying to erase his mind, a ferocious hangover. He momentarily experienced the disorientation of the nomad awakening in yet another strange place, and then the surreal events of his yesterday oriented him. His wristwatch informed him that it was six o'clock Sunday morning.

Best to slink away now, Roland thought. He would destroy the well upon his recovery tonight. He paused for a moment outside the door to breath the cool morning air, well aware that his pistol was missing.

"Ojo Solo sends his greetings." Godzilla appeared from behind

Intimidator. He spoke English in a pleasant bass.

Roland felt the panic of the previously abused. "Don't you ever sleep?"

Godzilla placed a large, battery-operated lantern on top of Intimidator that caught Roland in its glare. "I'm to deal with you for being a candidate for Magdalena last night."

"It didn't happen. Go trounce Ojo Solo. He set me up."

"I would welcome a chance to pinch Ojo Solo's head from his neck, but I'm well rewarded to participate in the Saturday candidate zip-izape." Godzilla advanced to a few steps from Roland.

Roland's headache increased as he surveyed the isolated junkyard, suddenly terrified to find himself on flatland, unhorsed and unarmed. "Don't you have the cause and effect confused by attacking me?"

"I've long thought so, but Ojo Solo pays a bounty for this work."

Roland leaped up and grasped a roof timber protruding from the adobe wall and hoisted himself to the flat roof a second before Godzilla made the quick capture move remembered. Roland stood and assured himself that he was beyond the reach of the huge ogre lurking below, comforted by being on the higher ground.

Godzilla dragged the better part of an automobile chassis against the house. The arrival of dawn enabled Roland to see that the roof was Francisco's weight training area. He stockpiled five pieces of heavy apparatus at roof's edge, dropping one on the chassis to rattle his saber.

"Is this a Mexican standoff, Godzilla?" Roland watched for a counter move. "That clatter should bring Francisco out to protect his property."

"Francisco the Good is tied up at the moment." Godzilla leaned against Intimidator. "He gets an ugly case of righteousness from time to time, not a gifted scum bag."

"Could I out-bid Ojo Solo?"

Godzilla sneered. "I doubt you can match his bounty, and it's regular work."

"Who were you before you became a frightener?"

"A frightener, that's a good one." Godzilla actually guffawed. "Two years ago, I owned my own health club in San Diego, a two-time Mr. Universe. I was a volunteer fireman, got this face in a fire. My customers couldn't stand the sight of me."

"Were you married?"

"Still am, and she and the kids are afraid I'll come home."

Roland picked up a hefty barbell. "It's nearing my breakfast time. I'll trade my freedom for a good job in the States with Roadways."

"Your interrogation tells us you can't even help yourself. You're a free lance maverick with no permanent address."

"What else do you do for Ojo Solo?" Roland dropped the barbell on the chassis to mark his territory while he searched for wiggle room.

"In political-correctness speak, I'm a bank security specialist, guarding all Libertad receipts placed in the Baptistery Bank. I distribute money or bartered goods between Magdalena, Ojo Solo, and Francisco in an equitable manner for their operating costs and protect the considerable balance. My services maintain honor and tranquility of a sort among the three boss thieves."

"Why do you do it?"

"It pays well for little work in a place as ugly as I am. Ojo Solo did it until Francisco caught him with his hand in the till. Now Ojo Solo has caught the Magdalena disease that gives men the night sweats imagining that she will come to them."

"Good thing you never caught that disease yourself."

Godzilla removed Roland's pistol from inside his coveralls and fired two bullets between Roland's boots. "The fire took my face, not my dick, so I sweat it out every night. Too bad you didn't puke last night, the men would've given you Magdalena and a ticket out of here. Now Francisco gets Intimidator to salve his guilt. He's getting ready to bug out for his Tres Rios hideout any day now."

"What do you get?" Roland asked.

Godzilla lifted the gun. "I get to shoot you, Roland, you arrogant, pretty-boy French prick."

The bullet struck Roland in the pit of his gut, knocking him back on the roof. He gazed up at the top of Cíbola mesa with profound longing and regrets. Why did his ancestors abandon the security of a high-mountain combe atop Mont La Breya to become horsemen, Zains? Neutrality, not assertive foresight, enabled them to be the first freemen of Europe. Roland always secretly wished that he could live his life in a little valley at timberline, grow an alpine garden, and be surrounded by a loving and caring family. He cried out from pain deeper than the bullet wound, because the alternate reward of Ludie's substantial dowry and handsome face and form would never be his.

Mistaking Roland's cry of sorrow for physical pain, Godzilla climbed to the roof and administered a coup de grace between his eyes, sending him to the final zipizape.

# PART 3
# GRAN ABUELA

# Chapter 9

Harold Mason hated to visit Roadways Company headquarters in Chapel Hill. The entire setting was much too informal and chaotic, lacking the dignified climate befitting a company of Roadways' financial standing. Several of the ever-present student protestors loitering about – even though it was Saturday when they should be carousing at a soccer match – had the effrontery to address him by his first name, demanding to know when he was going to stop abusing the old Papago women in the Sonora. Harold hated all big-business Anglo-Saxons in the United States for their smugness and continued belief in their invincibility. Why didn't the fools realize that they were only products of foul play and dumb luck during the colonial period wars? In due course, they would learn that their northern cousins were not yet defeated. "Roadways will soon be headquartered in Toronto," he thought, "and all will be placed in order."

He had already selected a site on the shore of Lake Ontario, which was well suited for an imposing brick building of his own design. The structure, featuring four imposing spires, would be his declaration of what a true Mason can accomplish. This bold masterwork would revenge him against his father, Master Jerric, who always touted himself as the ultimate Master Freemason. Harold would then surround himself with a proper Canadian support staff. None of the silly buggers from Chapel Hill would be invited.

Harold was also intent on a complete restructuring of all Roadways entities, once its name was obliterated and placed under The Mason Company logo. His expanded empire would champion the old, tried-and-true ways of male superiority in all matters. Such claptrap as equal opportunity in employment could be easily circumscribed in a multinational company with a myriad of geographically diverse operating locations.

The security agent called Patience gave him a cursory glance only, as usual, in the main reception areas. She accompanied him on an elevator to the third floor. Nary a word was spoken. Harold was not at all comfortable in her presence, a cold fish this one.

Harold spied Ludie working at her desk and paused before entering her office. She was dressed in the same drab, brown, mannish suit worn at their last meeting, and she was wearing those terrible brown walking shoes. This woman will have to improve her grooming, Harold mused. His trophy wife can't be a laughing-stock in Toronto. He noted, also, that Ludie's desktop's sole ornamentation was the black-framed photograph of her Great-Grandmother Mariah. It wasn't a flattering likeness of the old biddy. Her chin was much too firm, and her steel-gray eyes looked as if they could pierce armor plating.

Mariah's picture drew Harold's thoughts back to Master Jerric who, although dead for more than ten years, always loomed large in his life. From an early age, he had thought of his father as Master Jerric in a mocking manner, but had never dared to address him in this manner. Harold, the eldest son, had never been able to satisfy Master Jerric, no matter that he had performed each task assigned, many petty, to the best of his capabilities. Master Jerric had always pestered Harold about preparing himself to don the leadership mantle of the powerful Mason clan. Never in his lifetime had he approved of Harold's efforts or his accomplishments. Harold had sweated and suffered while his four siblings had stayed hidden away with his mother Rowena. He longed to forgo the detestable first son role and tuck himself safely inside the Mason family litter, escaping the curse of primogeniture. Rowena had accepted divorce without protest, never accorded the loving and caring she so richly deserved.

Ludie glanced up and saw Harold, frowned, and beckoned him into her office. "There you are Harold. You're late. We'll meet in the small conference room behind you, so I'll join you shortly."

Harold turned about and entered the drab windowless room furnished only with a round table and four chairs. Ludie had again relegated him to the way station for the powerless visitor. During Grethe's reign, he was always escorted into the spacious corner office, seated on a sofa with a favored view of the pine grove and fish pond, and served coffee and hot Danish. His stomach grumbled at the deprivation he suffered today. He decided to stand until Ludie entered, experience instructing him that he was rather ungainly while rising from low chairs.

Ludie entered, gave Harold a perfunctory nod, and seated herself at the table. "Thanks for coming to Chapel Hill on such short notice. I'm embarrassed to admit that I'm in over my head with the Cíbola mine shutdown project. Grethe must be spinning in her grave. Could you possibly go down there and bail me out?"

Harold was in near-shock at this first-ever sign of weakness from a Carter female. Was the young, pig-headed Miss Ludie finally discovering that she was incompetent to lead Roadways? Apparently so, and just too right. This turn of events offered some intriguing tactical and strategic possibilities. Master Jerric had taught him that chaos or corruption could be your friends if you were prepared to pounce.

"Before you reject me, please allow me to state my case." Ludie glanced down at papers spread on the table. "I've terminated my ill-advised engagement to Noah. I'm now sorry I sent him to Cíbola last

week to lend a hand down there, because he's made a mess of things."
She peered at Harold through smudged, black-rimmed eyeglasses and
favored him with her full attention. "Noah managed to get himself mis-
placed shortly after you saw him in Hermosillo. Evidently, he convinced Jorge to escort him on a silly search for a new gold deposit, a
juvenile attempt to salve his ego. Would you please return to Cíbola and
send him back to Josiah? With all the trouble I'm having managing the
business, I need Josiah here for a bit longer."

Harold sucked in his stomach and nodded with vigor. What an enjoy-
able duty it would be to humble the junior Chamberlain, the dilettante
do-gooder! The stallion that does not neigh should be castrated.

"That's grand of you," Ludie said. "And please watch out for Victor.
He's just being awful to me."

This is the ticket, Harold thought. This little filly is learning of the
need for the firm hand of a man. The rough hands of a Mason would
train her to the bit and the spur. But, he cautioned himself, be careful to
keep her in the docile, befuddled state she is now in, a much more exciting condition sexually for Harold's tastes. Master Jerric had always said
that old truths are the only truths, but he had used only the truths that
served his purposes. First wives are selected from within the clan to
continue the bloodline, while the prime function of second and third
wives is to enrich the clan. He would now direct Ludie to continue the
meeting in her office, with coffee and hot Danish, and lay down the law
on the absurdity of Mariah's feminist claptrap. Ludie was a dolt to
believe that she could capture a weak-willed, male ninny with property in this day and age.

Ludie glanced at her wristwatch. "Darn, I've got to go to my budget
meeting. Please join Josiah in the situation room. He's at your service."
She sauntered from the room with a listless wave of her hand.

* * *

"This is quite enough information, Josiah," Harold said. "I've made it my business to be well informed of all Roadways activities. But do tell me this, if you please. Weren't the dozen mining group project locations marked with black flags previously? I note that all Roadways locations are now designated in white."

Josiah fussed with his exhibits. "Ludie's orders, Harold. She said that it's no longer necessary to differentiate between them. Grethe enjoyed seeing her mining group operations on display."

"Roadways does own the controlling interest in all mining joint ventures for the moment." Harold looked about the cluttered situation room. "A number of changes will be forthcoming as soon as I return from Cíbola."

"Are you going to lift the blockade on Cíbola? The damned TV coverage is so embarrassing to Roadways it's hurting our capabilities to get new business. We may lose that huge road construction project in Turkey."

Harold savored this moment. Perhaps this toady could influence Ludie to his liking. "Is it indeed, Josiah? Then best you speak to Ludie about accommodating my terms. I simply wish controlling interest – seventy-five percent comes to mind – of the mining group. Further, I wish control of all Mexican road construction activities, which are to be included in my mining group."

"That's not wise." Josiah actually wrung his large hands in frustration, a certain sign of his descent from the lofty crisis intervention specialist pedestal Grethe had placed him on. "Roadways has long expertise in the Mexican road construction market. We've got the business and political connections. Your demands would place us at a competitive disadvantage at the very time that road construction opportunities are increasing."

"Roadways must accept new priorities in Mexico. Mining will be the moneymaker, and road construction a facilitator. Observe the Mason Company's Canadian strategic plan as the model. We were the successful bidder to construct roads into isolated, mineral-rich areas. Thus, others paid a hefty portion of the development costs for the mine sites we targeted."

Right on cue, Josiah looked very distressed. "That strategy isn't available in the United States." He pointed to a marker near Las Vegas. "And the Nevada gold mine will fail, because the unions will never permit treatment of workers similar to what occurred at Cíbola."

"I'll not attempt to tinker with the United States union-management scheme. The Nevada mine will be my training site for Mexican mines. The gold deposit is good, but not great. The mine's contribution will be the training of specialists to send to a projected fifty precious metal mine sites in Mexico." Harold eased back in his chair and patted his stomach in satisfaction. "And Mexico will become a springboard to invade Latin America's mineral wealth."

"But Victor will never permit such a strategy in Mexico."

"Not true," Harold said. "Victor simply wishes the price to be right for himself. He has no business leadership aspirations, so Cíbola is his desired model for participation with Roadways. Victor wishes to be a power broker only, making no financial investments for a significant portion of the profits. Accusations of gold theft are only his means to bring Roadways to the bargaining table, so I'll oblige him when at Cíbola."

Josiah startled Harold by pounding a large fist on the table. "Harold, I can't let you ruin Roadways' Mexican business relationships. I've got to protect Ludie until she gets on top of things. Why don't you back off while I go down to Cíbola and square things around. I'll do it quick-like, so Ludie won't be the wiser."

"Ludie has forbidden you to interfere at Cíbola, so I surmise that you would risk your financial future to search for Junior. A laudable intent, but very foolish at best. Recall that your retirement benefits can be denied if you take actions counterproductive to Roadways' profits. Do Junior a favor and give him room to fail. Growth follows young people's failures."

"I haven't observed you using that prescription for growth for your sons."

"Too true for I've no need," Harold said. "They're the descendents of a long line of Masons, secure in their knowledge that they'll succeed me in perpetuating the Mason clan in due course. Your Junior has never enjoyed such security."

Josiah bristled. "That's not true. I've had a successful career with many promotions and pay increases. He was well provided for."

"You're making my case." Harold enjoyed toying with this near-has-been. "Where are Junior's bricks and mortar to depend on when you're gone? Does he inherit your position? Certainly not. Have you inculcated him with your assertive crisis intervention skills? Obviously not, so where's his blueprint for success? What model does he use to structure his life?"

"I've done my best, given the opportunities available to me."

"But you've succeeded yourself into a failed relationship with Junior according to all accounts. You leapt through a unique window of opportunity to rise far above your station as a Chamberlain. You're now clinging to your position, reluctant to climb back down the promotion ladder. Let go, Josiah, because you're a specialist who has outlived your specialty, now nothing but a spent hard-charger ready for the glue factory. Your position will certainly not be replaced in my scheme of things."

Josiah ground his knuckles. "So you've made a special project to study me. Am I that dangerous to you?"

Harold chuckled, now amused. "Don't flatter yourself. You're most typical of a great many men of your generation, as is Junior in his own crowd. I surmise that your personal behavior is not to his liking, so you're being boycotted."

"Did Noah follow his mother into teaching, so he could have a structure to occupy?"

"Without doubt," Harold said. "In addition, he's trying to cope with the ambiguity the children of mixed marriages suffer. Is he to be a leader once follower?"

Harold left the situation room, leaving Josiah with hands clasped before him at the table. He would be wise to pray, for he had little else to rely on. Harold reflected with satisfaction that the man was certainly getting his comeuppance. All schoolyard bullies have the same mentality they take into later life. Once they determine what they desire, they tread over anyone in their path to grasp it, rupturing propriety and the natural order.

He had long since learned that the best way to defeat these hard-chargers was to take a circuitous route; slow but certain is the ticket. He was now bound for Cíbola to cement the stones in place with Victor that would wall Ludie into a corner that she could escape only by his bride-capture of her.

Jerric would soon be spinning in the grandiose mausoleum the gross lard-pot had built for himself, because the paradigm Harold designed for himself would win the day. Cunning would be his winning strategy, allowing him to avoid hand-to-hand combat by keeping to a sensible, safe path by the use of indirect, subtle methods. Grethe, the great manipulator, would be out-manipulated after all. And Master Jerric, who had professed to be a model of assertive leadership, would be exposed as a posturing charlatan.

Certainly, Harold mused, Master Jerric had considered himself to be a life-long member of the Freemason brotherhood, free to move from town-to-town without restraint by local guilds. Outside his home he had mouthed their principles of brotherliness, charity, and mutual aid. But he had never, ever, shared any of his professed beliefs with his eldest son.

# Chapter 10

Maru led the invasion of the high mesa Sunday night, her long walk ended after twenty years. She was born seventy springs ago on this mesa, before it was called Cíbola. Maru was at last back in her homeland, the place where her stolen property was captive. Even if all else was plundered and ruined, the little house held the spirits of the great loving and caring she once possessed. She would demand much to repossess little.

Yet another Anglo at guard at the forbidding iron gates enabled entry, believing pails and bundles those of cleaning women. Maru kept eyes lowered under the brim of her large, worn campesino hat to feign subservience, but Nita's babbling pulled the chubby man's nose from the papers he studied.

Maru made a distraction, hoping he also spoke Spanish. "Take care you shiftless old Papago woman. We must make sparkle the guest house."

The foolish Nita batted her eyes and wiggled her ass. The man scowled and returned to his papers, another Anglo pendejo. Maru walked past deserted mills and houses, refusing to glimpse her house on the rim of the mesa. Without hesitation, she led the way down into the awful mining pit, her path lit by the May Milk Moon, and rushed to the Great Corúa.

Nita was directed to place the sacred salt and beans at the pillar's base and go to her blankets across the roadway that spiraled down to the pit's bottom. With palms lifted to Milk Moon, Maru danced to feel Mother Earth through her bare feet. Her steps were defiant and possessive, but soon slowed to a pattern of supplication for the return of her house.

Maru retired to her blankets before the Great Corúa, because tomorrow the battle for a Great-Grandmother reservation would begin. The rape and abuse was ended, so the passive resistance of old Papago women was needed, their jobs by default and design. The ignorance of the Anglo at the gate won entrance, but Maru must find a way to harvest the hatred and greed of the Anglos and the Spaniards.

As Maru looked to the sky from her blankets, she saw the contrail of a jet from Tucson shooting south over the Sonora desert. Was this a sign from the Great-Grandmother? Had Maru brought Nita into a place for the dead only?

"Abuela Maru, where are you? I can't find your blankets." Yulla spoke Spanish instead of Papago because of her schooling – what a pity. Her accent approached that of an Anglo because of too much Anglo TV, another pity.

Maru summoned Yulla to her blankets, not dismayed that her nine-year-old granddaughter had escaped her mother, Habita, to join her. This loving rebellion must cease when the Roadways and Emblema big shots arrived. Only Maru, the leader of the old Papago women who coveted the ravaged mesa for their reservation, their sanctuary, must be at risk.

"You must not come to me again." Maru released Yulla's fat braid of black hair. She again marveled at the gift of this perfect granddaughter with wise woman potential, athletic grace, and a beautiful, strong face, her nine-year-old face.

"But, Abuela, it isn't fair. I can run here in ten minutes, and Milk

Moon told me to come to you."

Aeeii, Maru thought, this female child has the gifts, already using Maru against Maru. "Now, now, Yulla, do not use Milk Moon for your selfish purposes. She is very busy watching over Mother Earth nowadays, but she may glimpse your naughtiness from the corner of her eye. I must tell you why I have come here tonight."

"We always came to see you in Imuris," Yulla said. "Mamma and Papa were pissed when you and the other old Papago women blocked our road to the mesa. Now the TV news hounds from Tucson are showing them before their fires and little rock piles."

"I will tell you the Great-Grandmother myth that guides me. It foretells that old, wise Papago women must sacrifice themselves for their granddaughters."

Yulla made safe her notebook and pencil and snuggled against Maru. "Por favor, don't leave anything out. I'm old enough to know everything, especially things about sex."

Maru felt a pang of guilt at her willingness to tell Yulla her contrived myth. But her resolve to stay the path hardened when she thought of the many years invested in the repossession of the mesa holding her house.

The core of the myth had been told to Maru by her own grandmother. "In the beginning, the Great Mystery Power used loving and caring to create the Mother Earth and all the plants and animals living on her. Great Mystery Power made brown, white, black, and yellow people, but not many at first. Mother Earth gave the lands most call the Americas to the brown people, because they were her best friends. The Great-Grandmother, Sister Moon, and Father Sun helped the Mother Earth nourish the brown people in the Americas."

"Wait, Abuela, is this a myth or religious stuff?"

"They are the same thing, Yulla. Now, Great-Grandmother and Sister Moon favored the Hohokams, now called Papagos, because they lived in peace on the same lands for a thousand years and used the summer floods to irrigate their fields and grow beans, corn, and squash. Father Sun helped our Shoshone cousins in the north, sending them Old Man Coyote for their guidance. The Apaches are one of the Great Mystery Power's mistakes, so rattlesnakes watch over them."

Maru did not smile when Yulla peered into her face. Her grand-daughter must learn this fanciful myth and relate it to others. On this Maru's life depended. "Great- Grandmother claimed this mesa for her very own. She placed a Corúa, the great serpent, as guard of the Birth Spring that once flowed with abundance. A Corúa guards each Papago spring of significance. The Papago people were blessed with sweet water at their beautiful village atop the Great-Grandmother mesa. Nearby, on the desert floor to the north, was the people's summer vil-lage where they drank saguaro wine to excess to bring rain and grew their crops on the flood lands. Evil men now use this sacred place to prepare men for their journey to the United States for jobs, and steal their money when they return."

Yulla pondered for a moment. "But why does Great-Grandmother let these bad things happen?"

"Great-Grandmother watches over the cycles of birth, growth, death, and a rebirth of the people on this mesa. But now, the heart of our mesa is gone, the Birth Spring destroyed when Mother Earth's veins were cut. The poisons from the destroyed heart have killed the plants and the ani-mals on the flood lands. All was caused by the two horrible heart-rip-per conquistadors called Roadways and Emblema."

"Did Great-Grandmother know all this in the beginning?"

"The Great Mystery Power made the ending the same time as the beginning. All paths exist, and we are each to travel our true paths to find loving and caring. Great-Grandmother hides the truths in the myths. She will reveal true paths to those with strong hearts."

Yulla was as practical as her mechanic father. "Why did the Papagos leave our mesa?"

"When the white people came to the Americas, many Papago people gave their hearts to the soldier-priests who were very clever. They used a Holy Ghost to change Father Sun into a Father and Son who did the soldier-priests' bidding. The Papagos forgot the Great-Grandmother laws and wandered from her mesa. A people divided are a people conquered. The Apaches killed many of us, because the Papago wise women could no longer elect a Brother Cuckoo."

Yulla giggled. "What's a Brother Cuckoo?"

"He was the war chief chosen by the wise women from the peace-loving men in the fields to defend against Apache raids. After a Brother Cuckoo led us to victory, the wise women took him for the rituals to cure insanity. Only an insane person learns to excel in the killing of other people."

"How did the wise women cure the Brother Cuckoo's craziness?" Yulla asked.

"Aeeii, Yulla, the cure for the ancient heroes was to drink saguaro wine, have much sex in the moonlight with eager partners, and improve their pottery-making skills."

Questions ceased for a moment while Yulla reflected on this information. "Is Great-Grandmother punishing the Papagos because we're bad?"

"The Great-Grandmother does not judge good or bad. She warned that our hearts would be ripped out and eaten, but she loves the Papagos and longs for a Brother Cuckoo to recapture our mesa for a reservation."

Yulla shivered under the blankets. "Where's the Brother Cuckoo now?"

"Soon he will appear because many old Papago women at their fires and small Corúa shrines outside the gates are summoning him to defeat the conquistadors." Maru now spoke in a whisper. "Many years ago a brave, but foolish, man died where my blankets are and became a ghost spirit. He was your Grandfather Oidak. On that day, the Great Corúa appeared from the pit. It was foretold that Great-Grandmother would make this her shrine, and the mesa would grow a new heart. But a Brother Cuckoo must lead us. He will be handsome, strong, brave, and love you, Yulla."

Yulla was delighted. "That sounds exactly like my Papa. How wonderful!"

"Yes, you may be right. Tomas Mechanio would be a perfect Brother Cuckoo, truly a great honor."

Yulla slept with a smile on her lips. Milk Moon returned the smile. Before Maru slept, she pondered once more her myth-riddle. Could it create a pattern bringing her son-in-law, Tomas, to the Brother Cuckoo duties? Maru needed a strong man to confront other men in the male-dominated Sonora, so she transformed ancient wisdom to meet modern obligations. Tomas was uniquely qualified to intercede with Roadways and Emblema, if he has the cojónes.

* * *

Maru heard Habita approach the Great Corúa as the sun marked ten o'clock. She permitted her daughter to examine Nita's empty blankets before discovering her sleeping daughter and silent mother. She, too, would speak Spanish with the Anglo accent created by their TV.

"Mama, Yulla must leave now," Habita's fists were on her hips. "Tomas doesn't want the Anglos to know that you're her grandmother, for fear that he won't be allowed to go to Nevada."

"Tomas must calm his fears." Maru was not surprised. "No one will note that two old Papago women have invaded the mesa."

"Then why is Victor Emblema on his way to the mesa now to interrogate you? Explain this to me, you smarty pants."

Maru slowly arose from her spare bed of blankets. She had adopted this sleeping mode when she started her long walk, but Mother Earth demanded a higher price from her bones each year.

Habita had no patience with Maru, who would not enter the house Habita now occupied until she returned it to her. "Mama, look at this horrid hole you covet without the hate you feed on."

Gazing down into the deep, raw gash that remained after the machines tore the gold from the mesa, Maru eased the waistband of the jogging suit worn for sleep to help delay her visit to the worker's portable toilet across the roadway. "It took Roadways and Emblema thirty years to make this pit look like Sister Moon's craters. Papago fields could reappear in this awful wound if we are given the water from the well at the base of the mesa."

Habita rejected the program. "Mama, leave Tomas alone. He's worked so hard and all the Anglos admire him. He's won a job in Nevada, Señor Mason said so."

"I know no Mason."

"He now guards the gate because your old women have made guards and other workers quit the mesa."

Maru shrugged. "Mason is nothing but a chubby Anglo pendejo."

Habita stamped her foot. "You're a know-nothing and don't know it. Señor Mason is the Roadways official sent here to dispose of Cíbola, the third such man this week, but a true big-shot this one. He will construct a new gold mine in Nevada where Tomas hopes to work."

Maru retreated to pathos. "Your father made a woman of me on this mesa under a May Milk Moon. I gave birth to you alone screaming my joy. Your father was gnawed to death on this very ground, wailing our names. I want only a place for women to work and wait in safety, while the men go north across the despoblado and the border for jobs. This mesa is raped and diseased. Who could want it but old women?" She looked up at the high, canted rock pillar that loomed above them. "I will join your father's ghost spirit here at the Great Corúa if I fail. My blood will join with his."

Habita retrieved Yulla from the blankets. "I'm warning you to leave Yulla out of this scheme. It's the same old hate-hash with a couple of whistles and bells tossed in." She kissed Yulla. "Mama, you could get us all killed, because the old women are actually listening to you now. You can't mix your lame understanding of passive resistance with the Brother Cuckoo myth, Great-Grandmother wish-dreams, and Great Mystery Power hokum. You just want the house back that Roadways gave Tomas and me. Keep your daffy ideas to yourself when you meet with Victor in the maintenance building."

Aeeii, Maru thought, why does Habita have it all? She married for love. Oidak had forced himself into Maru for her father's favored fields on the flood land. No matter that he had claimed to be clowning about after drinking too much sequro wine. Rape was rape. She had made a decent mate of him; but when the macho fool had been eaten by the mining machines, she had been dispossessed of the house she had helped build for Don Josiah and Doña Sarah.

Yulla dressed and collected her notebook. "Mamma, will Tio Noah return today?"

"Hush, Yulla," Habita said. "We'll not bother Maru with Noah now. She's too busy being a busybody."

"But, Mamma, he and Jorge should have found the gold by now, and he said he would return, he's my only Tio."

Maru's suspicions were confirmed. The man at the gate with Francisco and his big machine was the little Noah she once cared for, grown large. "Be very careful, Yulla, when you are with Anglos who wish to be trusted. These are dangerous people."

"Abuela, I'm scared when you talk like that. Is Captain Guardia going to kill you and the old women?"

"Certainly not, so do not worry. I say these things only to excite people to give us a reservation. Guardia will take me to jail when we refuse to leave. That is the reason that I am the only old woman who guards the Great Corúa."

"And then the one thousand old women will flock to the jail in Hermosillo to demand justice," Yulla said. "That's what the Great-Grandmother myth promises, doesn't it?"

"It would seem so. Now, you be careful and stay away from all Anglos, particularly the son of the treacherous Doña Sarah and Don Josiah."

Maru soon walked up the road from the Great Corúa to the western rim and the terrible place that smothered the ancient winter village. It was like a boil on the brow of the mesa. Maru could not tolerate the view of the polluted western desert floor, so she hurried into the maintenance building. Only a few lights were on in the metal building with a vast square of concrete floor. The mills and mine were shut down, so none of the huge earthmovers remained.

Maru knew that Tomas had returned from escorting the last of the steel giants to the gold mine in Nevada. The Anglos paid him to assure that the machines' needs were understood by other maintenance mechanics. Tomas loved to be with machines and others who served them. It was this devotion to things mechanical that would make him difficult to recruit as Brother Cuckoo. Maru went to the mechanics' workspaces to engage Tomas without Habita's presence.

Harold, not Tomas, was among the benches and tool chests. "Ah, Maru, my little cleaning woman, I need tools to repair my automobile's trailer hitch." He spoke Spanish with precision, and no heart.

Maru appraised the self-important toad. "I thank you for letting me enter Cíbola." She was careful to keep her shoulders stooped and only glance fleetingly at Harold from under her hat.

"You're to depart this mesa as soon as you talk to Victor."

"Are there things I am to say to Victor that will help your cause?"

"Help me by keeping all the pathetic old women blockading the mesa in place until I dismiss them." Harold pointed across the building. "Wait in the conference room, have your little chitchat, and then depart with the foolish old woman you call Nita."

Maru entered the room, took a seat, and arranged her long denim dress so her scruffy desert boots were hidden. She decided to leave her hat on and not rise from her seat when Victor entered.

A man opened and closed the conference room door with care, walked directly to Maru, and bowed. "Buenos dias, Señora Maru, I'm called Victor Emblema. Por favor, may I be seated?"

Maru was prepared for an encounter with a churlish conquistador, sword on the ready. Seen up close, Victor was a graceful, handsome man with a full head of black hair brushed back from a wide forehead. He had less than forty years and appeared fit. The coat to his fine black suit was draped about his shoulders. He spoke Spanish in a lisping baritone.

"It's urgent that I meet soon with the TV reporters," Victor said. "I must learn from you why you've ambitions to create a reservation on this mesa? An Indian should never wish to be on a reservation."

"How can you know of reservations? Mexico has none. You have not given us even the meanest part of our own lands. Papagos have the second largest reservation of all tribes in the United States, more than four million acres."

"Exactamente! The Anglos don't wish to mingle with their Indians. They hide them away on reservations, so they can conceal their shameful acts. Mexicans embrace our Indians as brothers."

"My women tell me that Mexicans only embrace Indian sisters to make babies. They also say that Mexicans will couple with anything, even goats. Forgive them, for theirs is a hard life."

Victor jerked forward in his chair, shedding his coat and patrician manners. "Stupid old woman, how can you know of the shame inflicted on Indians in the United States and the enlightened policies of Mexico towards your people?"

"I learned as I wandered throughout Papago lands that straddle the border. My mother died in the Mexican Sonora from cancer, unable to receive one peso for care. I watched Papagos die on the reservation in Arizona, because they used their government bribes for drugs, rodeos, and drunken dances at Father and Son shrines. They, at least, could get medicines and a bed when dying."

Maru kept her eyes downcast and made her words halting. "If my women had a Great-Grandmother reservation, they would return to the ways of the ancient ones who valued each woman, man, and child in the tribe, gave others anything they could not consume, and revered the land they lived on. And they killed other people only when attacked. We wish this useless mesa and the water from the well to wait in safety while our men are in the United States seeking jobs."

"What's this nonsense about the restoration of the mesa being pre-destined?" Victor asked. "Do you know of this pagan folktale?"

"Many old Papago women know the Great-Grandmother myths. Myths always tell truths, but the truths are hard to find."

Victor turned at the door before departing. "What can you know of myths, old woman? You're confusing them with superstitious peyote trances. Continue your pitiful games for now while imprisoned on the mesa."

"I will never live anywhere but on our Great-Grandmother reservation which is to include the well that robbed the Birth Spring of its water."

"Ha, ha, you're truly a crazy harridan. That well is now mine. When there's again water atop this mesa, it's yours." Victor smiled with smugness. "I'll tell the TV reporters this now. But tell me, old crone, what would you do if I instructed the Federales to break heads or slit the throats of those blockading the mesa?"

"The smoke-fires would summon one thousand more women to join me for the massacre. The news hounds would make videos for the television in the United States. Roadways would lose its profitable projects in Mexico, and you would not share in their plunder."

Victor returned to hover above Maru. "I was correct in joining Harold to hurry the profits from this place. My father Don Carlos, God save his soul, was too solicitous of the peones welfare for today's business." He lingered. "What, no snide response, old hag? Roadways will be exposed for the greedy Anglos they have always been. Ludie Carter will yet beg me to be a business partner in Mexico."

"You will dishonor Don Carlos if you do not return the mesa to the Papagos. I was present many years ago when he stood with Don Josiah at the Birth Spring and made this pledge to us on his mother's Sacred Soul."

Maru laughed aloud when Victor leaped back in confusion and slammed the door behind him. Surely the furor she was creating would cause Roadways and Emblema to give the mesa and the well to the old Papago women and retreat. But a Brother Cuckoo must be recruited to intervene in her favor in this crisis of her creation.

* * *

After returning from her encounter with Victor, Maru watched Nita store the barter goods she had scrounged from abandoned shacks. Nita had joined Maru in the advanced guard to capture the mesa because she had too many sons, sons-in-law, and grandsons lazing about her home demanding her domestic labors. Her husband had long since died of exhaustion and tequila. Nita attended three shrine sites over the years to pray that her men would take the journey north to the United States for jobs, to no avail. So, Nita, to be separated from the shiftless lot, wished to be locked away on the mesa, where she lusted to scrounge at will.

Maru rested at the altar of the Great Corúa and pondered the real significance of the huge column of rock that protruded from the side of the pit, only a nub when first uncovered the day of Oidak's death. Maru thought of it as the tail end of a mythical sacred serpent that existed to perform its own cosmic functions for nature. Why could not the Great Corúa's remaining length descend into the mesa's bowels and enter the deep water well? It was a fanciful thought that excited the old women as she advocated the Great-Grandmother reservation, because the Corúa assured them that they, too, were part of nature, and still worthy of loving and caring.

Yulla suddenly appeared from behind the Great Corúa, notebook and pencil in hand. "Abuela Maru, Emilio the powder man, whom you call the smiling coyote, will soon come to the bunker. Nita should leave it now."

Maru started so that Yulla giggled. "Yulla, where did you appear from and what is this about a bunker?"

"I've taken the secret path from the rim to the Great Corúa. All news hounds like Christiane Anmanpour are mavericks knowing many secret, spooky paths. She's a great news hound, so soon she surely comes to Cíbola mesa."

"And the bunker, Yulla, what of it?"

Yulla pointed to a battered, pickup truck descending the roadway. "Emilio the powder man will tell you of it. I can't ride with him, because he doesn't like news hounds watching him."

Maru observed Emilio park the vehicle a short way below the Great Corúa, get out of the vehicle, and enter a doorway into the mountain. He was a weathered man with at least fifty years, perhaps handsome if not an Apache specialist. He soon exited from the bunker driving a front-end loader with Nita and her possessions in a container. Nita was shouting curse words in three languages.

Nita stood between Emilio and her meager possessions when Maru approached. "This man has stolen my hogan." She clutched a denim jacket to her bosom, fearing loss of her spoils.

Emilio wrested the jacket from Nita and placed it on the seat of the front-end loader. "The bunker is very dangerous, for there are unstable explosives in there."

"Only now does this Apache specialist give me explanations." Nita spit out the words Apache and specialist as curse words.

"This warehouse bunker goes deep into the mountainside." Emilio paid no heed to Nita. "A great hole would appear in the mesa if it exploded."

"But now I will have nothing of importance." Nita gathered her possessions. "Maru has the Great Corúa." Her eyes lit on the toilet. "That will be mine."

Yulla busied herself writing in her notebook. "Abuela, I forgot to tell you that Papa must talk to you at our house."

Maru took Yulla's hand and started the climb to the rim, steeling herself to approach her house. She went directly to the patio in the rear, having sworn never to enter until she repossessed it. Habita and Tomas were seated on a bench.

Habita wore a nasty face. "Harold now says Tomas can't go to Nevada, because Emilio told him that you're Tomas' mother-in-law."

Maru remained standing with Yulla. "I will go to him and shame him. Such cowardice!"

"You've really stepped into it this time." Tomas was very dour.

"I did not wish to risk your excellent reputation." Maru needed this lie to snare Tomas as Brother Cuckoo. He could be led to water, but he was reluctant to drink.

"Abuela, have supper with us," Yulla said. "You can sit by me."

"No, it is not possible to stay near this house longer. I will share the tortillas with Nita."

"But, Abuela, she's having supper with Rosa who prepared too much food for the guest house now that Tio Noah and Jorge have departed. Emilio has invited all on the mesa to attend."

"Yulla tells me that you do wish my help for a loco plot to repossess Cíbola, Maru." Tomas controlled his agitation well. "Forget it. I'll meet with Harold after Emilio and Rosa's supper to persuade him to send me to Nevada in spite of your far-fetched reservation scheme."

Maru admitted some pride in her son-in-law. Tomas was of average height, but his shoulders were broad and arms heavily muscled. His generous, black moustache strengthened his handsome face framed by shaggy black hair. Habita said he was a gentle lover. Was this praise or complaint?

"I have brought the women to the mesa so Roadways and Emblema will give us a Great-Grandmother reservation," Maru said. "Harold will appease us if you reason with him. You must do this for the dispossessed Papago women."

Tomas was infected with the Anglo disease of excessive rational thinking. "Your fascination with myths caused you to make a tactical error. You've created exactly the opposite effect you wish. Harold's delighted that you brought the Papago women to Cíbola, so he can threaten Roadways with their bloodshed. This, and the environmental mess, could force the Mexican government to deny Roadway's new business opportunities. Passive resistance sounds noble around the campfires, but a man like Harold will make the area outside the gates a Papago killing field for gold."

Maru assumed a look of concern. Tomas was inching his way to the water hole, so now he must thirst for fairness for dispossessed Papagos.

"Por favor, listen and learn, Maru," Tomas said, "a struggle is taking place over what's called the North American Free Trade Agreement, or NAFTA, that has politicians fighting over business profits and employment in the United States, Mexico, and Canada. Roadways desires the Mexican government to award them projects without the participation of Emblema Compañia. Roadways made a great mistake at Cíbola mesa many years ago that they're sworn not to repeat, allowing Don Carlos to be their partner without contributing money to build or operate the gold mine."

"But why did they permit Don Carlos to do this thing?" Maru continued her dumb-cluck role.

"This was the price Don Carlos extracted to grease the palms of the Mexican Federal officials to award the gold deposit to Roadways. A United States company couldn't be a majority owner in Mexico. Roadways found a way to rid itself of the cost and the embarrassment, using technology to deplete the gold ore deposit in the last few years instead of the many more years we hoped to enjoy."

Tomas permitted himself a smile of superiority. "There's nothing Victor won't do to make Roadways continue to pay him black money. You've blundered into a trap. Too bad the Great-Grandmother didn't give you a warning. Evidently she doesn't, after all, know all the endings and beginnings."

"If you will not help us, I will die at the Great Corúa, the completion of my life's circle." Maru avoided Yulla's gaze. "Will you force Yulla and Habita to slink away with you to Nevada? Will you hide behind your machines while the conquistadores massacre Papago women? Our people are being destroyed by the conquistadores, so the old Papago wise women are calling you, Tomas, to be their Brother Cuckoo."

# Chapter 11

Harold enjoyed the hike down to the bottom of the mining pit among the jumble of roads, embankments, dirt heaps, and boulders. But he paid little heed to the roadway or his surroundings as he hammered out a most satisfying agreement with Victor, who was a paragon of affability while focused on a business mission. By the time they arrived at the bottom of the pit, Victor bought Harold's entire program, proving himself to be an Hispanic lightweight.

Once Harold seated himself on a boulder and let his eyes trace the spiral path they had descended, he realized that his easy victory would be at a high price, his painful return trip. How could this be accomplished with dignity in his new black boots that were bedeviling his feet? For the moment, he watched Victor strut about exploring his surroundings. He wasn't properly garbed for the trek, as was Harold, but indicated no physical stress whatsoever. He removed his fine jacket from his shoulders and executed credible veronicas, the fop.

Victor did have one towering attribute in his favor, Harold mused. His companionship was far superior to that of Roland, who was reported to be lurking about in the Sonora, undoubtedly dispatched by Josiah to rescue the feckless Junior. Harold permitted himself a shudder, because he would never dare to be alone in this forlorn place with Roland, a reprehensible Frenchman utterly lacking in principles. He determined to invite Guardia back to Cíbola for his protection.

Master Jerric had always ranted at him that a Mason clan leader must have large stones to lead, always voicing the male obsession to be aggressively virile. When a young man, Harold had dismissed Master Jerric's macho ranting, because he had deduced that he was speaking from ignorance, unable to view his own undoubtedly diminutive wanker and stones concealed by his gut.

To distract himself, Harold reviewed his business coup in his mind. First off, Ludie was now totally out-flanked by his new alliance with Victor. During their descent into the pit, they had agreed to combine their shares of various joint ventures to gain a controlling interest of Roadways road construction and mining activities throughout Mexico. Of equal importance, Victor had placed Harold in full control, deserting Emblema's long alliance with the Carters. Victor evidently decided that when you discover you're riding a dead horse, the best strategy is to dismount.

Harold chuckled, because Victor's major tactical error was to permit his excessive, foolish respect for his father, Don Carlos, to convince him soon to return the mesa to the old Papago women for, of all ridiculous things, a so-called Great-Grandmother reservation. No wonder Anglo-Saxons always out-think and outflank Hispanics. They've few positive father-figure fixations.

Further, Harold reflected, Victor traded him his share of Cíbola's ore processing facilities for use at the Nevada mine in exchange for the water in the deep well. A good-news-bad-news scenario in Harold's view. Victor owned a precious well, but it was smack in the middle of the most despicable piece of geography imaginable. Resisting an urge to remove his boots and massage his feet, Harold consoled himself by reflecting with satisfaction that the spurious gold theft furor was to be quieted. Victor no longer intended to jail Jorge in order to perpetuate his foolish claim of a gold theft, not now needing Ludie's permission to make his company an effective partner in Mexican road construction projects. Harold no longer needed, or desired, the old Papago women's blockade to pressure Ludie for his own purposes, so they would be driven away. Shortly, the TV news hounds would retreat from a tranquil Sonora, according Harold considerable accolades for his statesmanlike conduct, and placing him in good stead for future successful NAFTA negotiations.

"So, Harold, we've what Anglos call a done deal." Victor stood before Harold and slowly pivoted about to examine fully the mammoth excavation. "As agreed, those dispossessed from the mesa will be returned to their homes, and this pit will someday have gardens. Perhaps some menial work can be discovered to occupy the women while their men seek work in the United States. The news hounds will record the progress to Emblema Compañia's greater glory."

"Roadways will also benefit," Harold said. "Should we decide for Ludie that it will contribute capital funding to restore homes and shops?"

"But of course." Victor was well pleased with himself. "And Mason Company will undoubtedly wish to participate."

"Curb your enthusiasm." Harold removed himself from the boulder. "Next you will request me to join you in restoring Libertad as a shrine site. But you must protect the well, the most critical element in the Great-Grandmother reservation's success and our escape from this God-forsaken hell-hole." He allowed Victor to precede him on the climb out of the pit, determined to acquit himself well.

Although eager to plan his announcement of the Great-Grandmother reservation, Victor waited for Harold one-third of the way to the mesa's top at a service plaza gouged into the hillside. "What's the function of this metal building and the hole in the hill with a pad-locked door?"

While regaining his breath, Harold pretended to ponder. "The building's a warehouse for equipment spare parts and the door protects an explosives bunker locked to prevent entry because Cíbola remains a dangerous place until all explosives are removed. Jorge was very careful to guard all assets, proving that you were indeed wise to rescind your accusations that he stole gold."

Victor smiled and shrugged. "The accusations served their purposes. My chief accountant suspected shortages, so accusing him warned of my vigilance, always wise when dealing with a Catalan. My most recent accusations have produced a most satisfactory alliance with you, resulting in a reduction of my executive duties which I highly value."

"As soon as Jorge recovers from his mania to discover another Cíbola in the Sonora, I'll hire him for the Nevada mine," Harold said. "His technical expertise is first-rate."

"Be reminded that I do not wish Jorge to remain in Mexico. Guardia, ever fascinated by crimes and criminals, believes that Jorge may well have stolen some of Cíbola's gold." Victor pointed to the explosives bunker. "The good captain has offered the premise that Jorge could easily pilfer small amounts of the richest ore each day and conceal it in a secure place such as the bunker. He believes that perhaps Emilio was in some manner his accomplice."

"Spare me the idle gossip of the local constabulary. As soon as I marry Ludie, I will put an end to all loose ends and bring order within Roadways. It is abundantly clear that she needs and desires my firm leadership style at the helm of Roadways."

Victor's buoyant mood was undiminished. "I'll follow with interest your pursuit of Ludie. However, beware that your success here today could be your downfall. Your very strength could become a liability in your efforts to capture Ludie as a bride." He unnecessarily brushed back his heavy hair with both hands. "Maybe I'm the perfect match for her because I've much property and no aspirations to master it." He laughed, enjoying his joke.

To Harold's relief, Victor apologized profusely for hurrying away and strode up the road to his waiting limousine and departure from Cíbola, a pea-brain on a fool's errand. But as Harold trudged up the road, his thoughts returned to Guardia's gold theft theory presented by Victor. The damnable dandy planted doubts in his mind. Why had Jorge agreed to work at Cíbola when he had been offered much higher salary and generous profit sharing elsewhere? And, come to think about it, why had he insisted on removing Harold's gold wagon guards from the ore extraction area? Such musings served to quicken Harold's pace, which produced much perspiration, a monstrous thirst, and a blister on his left foot.

As Harold peered up the road in the lengthening evening shadows, he felt a stab of fear in his gut, the return of an old malady. He had exposed himself to dangers, finding himself unarmed and unattended by corporate flunkies in a foreboding place where he had savaged the lives of many. What had possessed him to make this tactical blunder? Master Jerric, clutching his ponderous belly, must now be guffawing with glee in his mausoleum, if he still resided there instead of a special, hellish place reserved for tyrants. Harold rarely requested divine inter-cession, reserving this unreliable tactic for those times when he was in immediate physical danger. Please, God, Harold thought, make Master Jerric's punishment worse than mine. He was trapped on a high mesa in the Sonora surrounded by hostile natives and a despicable Frenchman free-lancer who was invading his newly-conquered domain intent on capturing the bride long targeted for his own rape.

When Harold finally made his limping approach to the rock pillar the locals called the Great Corúa, he saw Maru's witless companion called Nita seated near the base of the intrusive rock. She waved a can-teen at him, and his thirst and pain drew him to her. Nita arose as Harold approached. She wore a large shawl of a most disagreeable shade of green, centered by a yellow lightening bolt bordered in black. The shawl dragged on the ground as the short, plump woman with hennaed hair minced toward him. She winked as she handed him the canteen.

Harold was unable to refrain from chugging the water. Clutching the canteen, he then accepted the seat she offered him, any port in a storm, or a desperate need for water to survive.

Nita smiled and rearranged the lightening bolt to favor her breasts. "My name's Nita of Imuris. I'm one of the two brave women demanding this mesa for our reservation. Perhaps we can go to your quarters for coffee and cakes after you rest from your climb from the pit. I, too, am very tired and deserve a bed, and food, and drink, but I'm yours for as long as you wish."

Harold removed his left boot and sock to reveal a badly blistered heel. "Too bad you don't have the healing skills to assist me."

Nita laughed. "I've five sons and too many grandchildren. Who tends them after knife fights, falling in cooking fires, and scorpion stings? Mother Teresa."

At first, Harold thought he was merely buying time to rest, so he could enter the guesthouse with some semblance of dignity. But, then, he understood that he might be able to barter with Nita for information essential to his now urgent need to learn if Jorge had hoodwinked him. He struggled to his feet and gestured for Nita to be seated. "Por favor, Señora Nita, be seated. I apologize for my poor manners. Tell me the significance of the lovely shawl you wear."

With a look of astonishment, Nita seated herself with surprising grace, head held high. "Muchas gracias, Señor Harold. This shawl was purchased at a Papago sacred shrine site, for it reminds us of the waters brought by the rain and lightening storms and held in our sacred springs." She looked up at the Great Corúa. "Maru, who's my assistant, believes that praying at this great serpent shrine site may inspire you, Señor Harold, to grant us water from the deep well. She's not too clever, so you must forgive her the foolish things she does at this place."

"What things does she do, Nita?"

Nita pointed to a sheltered nook at the base of the pillar. "The usual useless supplications such as placing salt and corn on the ground and then falling face down in the priest-prone, cross-like position affected at shrine sites. As you can see, she's not a well woman and must be forgiven for her loco demand for a Great-Grandmother reservation. I humor her on this foolishness, for she's lost her appetites for sex, unlike myself."

Suddenly, the girl called Yulla appeared from behind the Great Corúa, a notebook in hand. "Nita, Abuela Maru told you not to wear her lightening shawl, she will be pissed." She appraised Harold. "Rosa is looking for you to ask if you wish your supper before the fiesta tonight."

"Scat, you little pest!" Nita said. "How did you get here?"

Yulla stood her ground. "I came down the smiling coyote's secret path behind the Great Corúa. It's a neat path, but you shouldn't try to climb it, Nita." She reappraised Harold. "Perhaps Harold can after he rests and puts his boot on."

"What's a smiling coyote, Yulla?" Harold now thirsted for additional information from any local. "Is it one of your pets?"

"No, no, silly, the smiling coyote is Emilio, the powder man. He keeps his explosives in the bunker beneath us and the bunker down in the pit at the service plaza. He uses both bunkers to give himself make-work."

Nita carefully folded the shawl and placed it on a nearby bedroll. "What're you doing here in my bedroom, little pest? Go to your house right now, and tell your mamma that she's looking for you."

Paying scant attention to Nita, Yulla addressed Harold. "I'm checking on Emilio's new padlock on the bunker. It's the third padlock in five days." She walked down to the heavy door in the hillside.

Harold was one step behind her, and Nita was his shadow. "When did Emilio change the locks, Yulla?"

"I'll check my news hound notes." Yulla flipped through her note-book. "Last Thursday, after Jorge loaded his truck in this bunker, Emilio placed a combination padlock on the door, a new, neat one. But when Roland arrived to get the Intimidator Saturday morning, Emilio put another old lock that needed a key on the door, and put another bolt on each of those three hinges. And now, Harold, when you arrived yester-day, he put the combination padlock back on, very curious."

"Are you fascinated by padlocks?" Harold asked.

"No, no, I'm an apprentice news hound, and I must find out why Emilio changed the padlocks since Jorge left. Always before, this was Jorge's bunker, and he always used the same old padlock. So did Emilio, but Jorge didn't know it."

"And the man you call your Tio Noah, what padlocks did he use?"

"Tio Noah didn't care about padlocks. He's a detective sent to Cíbola to find clues about stolen gold. I think he had too many clues but no suspects. He's no Columbo." Yulla nodded to Harold. "I'll tell Rosa you won't be ready for your supper for at least an hour. You should go to your bed early tonight."

Harold watched Yulla scamper up the roadway and disappear behind the Great Corúa. "Senora Nita, is that child truthful?"

"Drunks and children always tell the truth." Nita retreated to her throne at the Great Corúa.

Harold placed his new, khaki safari jacket and broad-brimmed hat in Nita's lap. "Please tell me what you know of this Emilio fellow, Nita. Anything at all."

Nita donned the hat, folded carefully the jacket, and looked at Harold, clearly waiting for more loot.

With reluctance Harold parted with his gold penknife and money clip holding at least two hundred dollars Canadian. He then outwaited Nita.

"Emilio is a bad, bad man," Nita said. "The only one on the mesa I fear. He's an Apache specialist who should've been among the first to go elsewhere for work, but he got into poor Rosa's panties so he could lurk about." She crossed her eyes and made the sign of the cross. "An Apache rattlesnake who's also a cunning coyote is powerful evil medicine. The more you sift Emilio's shit the worse it smells." She then retreated to a portable outhouse across the roadway.

Aside from being much too graphic for his sensibilities, Harold believed the information gained from Nita might well be a bargain. He felt a surge of excitement at the prospects of capturing some raw gold on his own accord. This was what being Cíbola bound was all about, wasn't it? He would yet silence Master Jerric's interminable nagging by demonstrating that he, too, could wrest golden plunder from the Sonora merely by the manipulation of the local yokels. He would summon this Emilio fellow to the top bunker and demand an explanation for his shenanigans. After all, Harold was the new top dog in the Sonora. Cunningness would yet win the day while assertive bunglers like Roland prance about on their imagined steeds. May he fall on his lance.

# Chapter 12

Maru was eager for her blankets at the Great Corúa after the late supper at the guesthouse. The unexpected largesse of Emilio permitted the few occupants of the mesa to enjoy a small fiesta. Maru had two glasses of wine and Nita many. At ten o'clock, Emilio declared that he would take food to Harold at the gate. Tomas departed soon after to plead with Harold that he be allowed to tend the giant machines in Nevada.

The Milk Moon told Maru that it was nearing midnight when she approached the Great Corúa. She congratulated herself for the excellence of her carefully constructed persona. Tomas explained events of her own creation, as if she were a foolish old woman. He thought her befuddled mind was so clouded by myths that she had no knowledge of NAFTA and the dynamics at work on each side of the stupid border between Mexico and the United States. The young firebrand social worker at the Arizona Papago reservation lent Maru books to read, while Maru studied her artful use of passive resistance to improve the lot of women and children.

Emblema and Roadways would now combat each other in the public eye of television, Maru thought. With Brother Cuckoo's male intercession, their eventual compromise would be Maru's Great-Grandmother reservation. Por favor, let this be so. The two conquistadores were

restricted in their maneuvering by political boundaries. Maru had no
such constraints. Papagos were once dispersed throughout the broad
reaches of the Sonora desert. Disparate treatments made Victor's arguments about reservations a mockery. Fewer than six hundred Papagos
live on the Mexican side of the border, while more than ten thousand
claim reservation status in the United States.

Gazing up at the Milk Moon, Maru raised a fist. Without pity, guilt,
or shame, she drove herself and manipulated the Papago women, her
family, and all others to repossess her property and avenge Oidak. They
had stolen him from Maru in his prime and shamed his name, after she
had suffered his bride-capture, borne his child, and performed faithful-
ly wifely duties. And, also, she had tolerated his self-assigned role as
tribal trickster. Buffoons are difficult to live with twenty-four hours
each day. Roadways had praised Oidak as the brave warrior of the con-
veyor belt oilers until he had been eaten by their machines. Then, only
then, had he been condemned for unsafe conduct, his death benefits
denied, and his widow dispossessed from her favored house.

Maru roused herself from her poisonous thoughts. She would attend
the Great Corúa on this last night of the May Milk Moon in full. To
recruit votaries, the benefitting clergy must attend a shrine. The Great
Corúa glowed softly in the light of the Milk Moon. What a pity that the
many women huddled outside the mesa were not here to witness this
great wonder.

But halt. Is the shrine being attended? Or is that the drunken Nita in
a priest-prone, cross-like sprawl before the shrine? The old ass had too
much wine while wearing Maru's lightening shawl that she again had
snatched without permission. Nita must be sleeping, the souse.

Maru bent and touched a shoulder to find that it was Emilio. He was
not breathing, none whatsoever. His head was so bloodied and twisted,
a broken skull, surely. And his mouth and nose were stuffed with white
flakes. Could that be cocaina? Aeeii, no, not the mafiosos here. But wait,

this is salt. Yes, the sacred salt on the altar is scattered.

Too much chaos, Maru thought. Who caused this effect? She felt neither pity nor elation in the Apache specialist's death. She had seen too many Papago dead in their own vomit at the shrine sites during her long walk. As she turned to flee, Maru's eyes caught the glint of silver metal under Emilio's left knee. She retrieved the object and was horrified to find it to be the El Jefe wrench, Tomas' great grand prize, smeared with blood.

Maru had made Tomas thirst for blood, so he killed Emilio for revealing to Harold his relationship to Maru. Her Brother Cuckoo has wasted his fury on a failed job opportunity in Nevada. No wonder he did not return to Rosa's party. Maru cried out Oidak's name and hid under her blankets, clutching the El Jefe wrench.

All the remainder of the night, Maru was silent, staying under her blankets pretending to sleep when Nita finally found her own blankets. Nita arose at sunrise to pee and stumbled across Emilio's body. She rushed up the road to tell of her important discovery to someone of importance, always starved for attention. Maru crept from her blankets and tossed the El Jefe wrench into the toilet. Federales would soon search and scatter their belongings, but they would not fish in the shitter. This was women's work.

In less than an hour, Nita returned to the Great Corúa riding with Harold in a giant red machine Tomas called a sports utility vehicle. Harold left the vehicle and strode to Emilio's body. Nita followed, wearing Maru's lightening shawl. She winked at Maru in her blankets.

Harold waited for her with patience. "Now, Nita, tell me your story. What time did you discover Emilio?"

"At sunrise." Nita spied Harold's gold watch. "I should be rewarded with a watch, so I would know these things."

"Did you see anyone else?"

"Uggh, such a headache, it wasn't possible." Nita rubbed her temples. "I was near to fainting, a frail, sensitive woman."

Harold persisted. "Any sign of a struggle?"

"No, no, he was so peaceful as he lay like a priest accepting – well, whatever they accept when they humble themselves before an altar." Nita noted Harold's confusion. "I'll show you how it was." She removed the shawl, spread it on the dirt, and lay facedown on it, head twisted, mouth agape, and arms outstretched.

Maru was furious at Nita. She was consorting with the Anglo and wallowing about on Oidak's shawl, the last gift he had presented to her. Awful as it was, she could not let it suffer such abuse. Poor Oidak, he had spent too many of their pesos for the horrid shawl when he visited the old shrine site north of the mesa many years ago. Maru must save the shawl. She moved quickly to Nita and whacked her fat ass repeatedly until she rolled from the shawl. Enough is enough.

Nita struggled to her feet. "Maru, you're a selfish bitch. I'm now telling Harold some truths about you, always hogging all of the attention."

"Do not tell Anglos anything, Nita," Maru said.

Harold approached Nita and placed his hand on her shoulder. "Nita, you're telling me lies about Emilio's murder, aren't you?" He took a silver liquor flask from his back pocket and held it before Nita's eyes.

"How did I lie?" Nita licked her lips. "How can I tell the truth you require?"

"Tell me who murdered Emilio, or I'll send you to the prison in Hermosillo."

"May I hold the flask for a moment?"

"Of course."

Nita removed the cap, sipped, recapped and placed the flask in her bodice. "Would I win also a lunch with wine if I tell you a truth? I would do this for my family's honor."

"The flask, lunch, and wine will be yours."

"Tomas killed Emilio," Nita sidled behind Harold. "He did this because Emilio robbed him of his job in Nevada by telling you that Maru is his mother-in-law." She quick-stepped across the roadway and locked herself in the toilet.

Maru watched with fascination the spectacle of Harold making a ninny of Nita in cold calculation. She was fascinated with her agile mind and grit in the horrid wasteland of the pit. Nita was ever ready for the next roll of the dice by those who never let her hold them. Unwittingly, she had just awarded Maru a Brother Cuckoo and, with careful management, perhaps her Great-Grandmother reservation.

Harold opened the back hatch of his vehicle. "Tomas will be taken to the jail in Hermosillo, Emilio to the morgue. Maru, go pry Nita from the toilet, because you two and all of your possessions are going to the maintenance building."

* * *

Maru was besieged with rebellions from all sides the following morning. Many more Papago women, bringing their men and children, gathered at the mesa because a Brother Cuckoo, Tomas, had risen and killed Emilio, a hated Apache specialist. Maru accepted no guilt, because she was only leading the stupid Tomas to a sip of water in her passive resistance pool, not a plunge into a blood bath

Habita shunned Maru for accepting Tomas' guilt, insisting he had retired to his bed. Habita has too long enjoyed the good life, Maru mused. Marriage to Tomas enabled her to live in Maru's house. Let her now feel the grief of losing her man. She would have no one to love and care for her and would experience the rejection and shame of being shunned by her own people. Then she would understand Maru's need for taking her long walk, searching for the path leading to a return to a loving and caring she craved.

The enriched Nita and bereaved Rosa quit the mesa, telling all that Harold would soon oust the arrogant Maru, so Maru was isolated from all but Yulla. Harold assured the news hounds that all was tranquil, and soon Victor would receive all news hounds in a gracious house in Hermosillo to make an important announcement.

Maru said nothing of the El Jefe wrench and found herself plotting to use Tomas' rash act to her further advantage. In her estimation, more truths should be known than said. She had desired that Tomas become a Brother Cuckoo, or close enough, by asking the Roadways people he chatted with about machines to reason with the Emblema people. But her Brother Cuckoo was a stupid goose to kill Emilio, although the effects were promising. Tomas killed Emilio because of the cursed male pride. The same awful conceit that made Oidak become the warrior of the ore conveying belts, waving his oil can like a war club, the old fool. If only Tomas had locked away his El Jefe wrench, she would not know he killed Emilio. Tomas was so proud when he had won the big contest ten years ago and been awarded the excellent adjustable wrench from Toledo engraved with "El Jefe," for he was the best, the boss, of all mechanicos.

Maru halted at a boulder cluster on the pit rim to search for Yulla at her favorite haunt. Yulla must again consult her notebook and report on the many events told by the TV.

"Abuela Maru, there you are, and I need your help." Yulla dashed up the roadway from the Great Corúa, clutching her notebook in one hand and a rock in the other. "Harold's mad at me for being Christiane Anmanpour. I asked him why he took the El Jefe wrench from Papa's workbench. He chased me into the spooky bunker shouting Anglo swear words." Yulla fell into Maru's arms amidst the boulders. "I slipped out and locked him inside his red automobile, bashing at the door."

Maru pulled Yulla behind a boulder, stroked her hair, and looked down the roadway for the offending Harold. At that instant, the entire Great Corúa toppled forward on the roadway accompanied by a tremendous explosion and a fireball. Then a massive rumbling shook the ground, and the Great Corúa and all things about it seemed to rise and then fall back onto themselves to form a gigantic avalanche ripping down through the spirals of the roadway.

* * *

Maru walked to the boulders overlooking the pit to observe again the miracle in progress. The massive explosion of twenty-four hours ago caused great sorrow and loss, but amends were underway. Gone was the Great Corúa. In return, the Great-Grandmother energized the Birth Spring, drying the well at the mesa's base. Water gushed from the deep orifice, cascading down until it encountered sound roadway. It then spiraled down to the bottom forming Lake Oidak, the name chosen by Yulla.

Tomas, the Brother Cuckoo, drew Papagos from throughout all the Sonora to champion the women's cause. The news hounds then reported that Victor had granted a Great-Grandmother reservation to the old Papago women, another miraculous happening. Maru puzzled out that Harold desired to destroy the Great Corúa to rid himself of the old Papago women and the TV newshounds, so he killed Emilio with the El Jefe wrench when he was discovered placing explosives at her shrine site, blowing himself to bits with his red vehicle. The Cíbola gold fever had harvested two more victims, a chubby Anglo pendejo and an Apache coyote specialist.

Maru stared at the waters from the Birth Spring that had risen to a rebirth. The afternoon sun caused shimmering that created an hypnotic effect. She longed to join this force and cease her struggle. Was not the ending decided in the beginning? Maru was invited to the peaceful oblivion of a completion of her life's journey. She had washed her own parents' bodies and had placed them in the sands when they had fallen from the western face of the mesa while on a favored path. She was not yet fourteen years old, but these loving and caring rituals had initiated her womanhood. A self-propelled ritual would place her on the spiral path down to the waiting essences of Oidak and the loving and caring due her.

With great effort, Maru blinked away the trance. She was fascinating herself with her own myth making. Oidak's ghost spirit was not lurking about. The old fool had been doing the hot-dogging with two beers under his belt and gotten chopped up. A clown playing childish games had lost her house. Time to quit playing hocus-pocus with his death, Maru thought, and give the Great-Grandmother myths a rest.

"Abuela, shame on you for standing too close to the edge." Yulla tugged at the back of Maru's dress.

Maru inched away from the Great Mystery Power's false gateway. She must now reveal truths to Yulla of her shameless, selfish manipulations. "Granddaughter, I was wrong to tell you lies of my belief in Great-Grandmother myths. I lusted to take advantage of the Papago women who shamed and shunned me when Oidak died. The women do not believe me, but they long to believe in the Great Mystery Power. But, Yulla, there is no Great Mystery Power. The mystery is that people can believe in a greater power. The Great-Grandmother myths are only the cud-chewing of dispossessed old women like myself."

Yulla's eyes were troubled. "But why are thousands of Papago women, men, and children now outside the gate clamoring to see the miracle of the Birth Spring's rebirth on the Great-Grandmother reservation? Is the Brother Cuckoo another of your lies?"

Maru paused to assure that she was speaking from her true heart, craftiness being her craft for too many years. "No, no, that is a truth passed down from our ancestors. At some time in our past, a brave man saved the Papago people from an Apache attack. This became a myth telling a truth."

At this moment, Maru knew herself to be cursed, a sick, sick thing. She could not tell the truth of Harold's murder of Emilio, because Tomas would be freed. Tomas must remain the Brother Cuckoo, so the Anglos would not withdraw her reservation and her house. In the Sonora not even murder, or innocence, can be wasted.

She stood with Yulla and viewed the birth of Lake Oidak. "Each of us must find and follow our own path to find our truths. We will forget the deaths that happened here and speak of the great loving and caring we still possess. Your Papa sacrificed himself to the Federales so the Papagos can possess the mesa. You and your Mama may live with me in my house."

"The news hounds say Papa will be twenty years in jail to cure his murder sickness." Yulla leaned against Maru. "He can return to Mama and you in the Great-Grandmother reservation's fields after his twenty-year journey. But I can't stay."

"Yulla, you are too young to leave your home. This will be an ideal place to live and work."

"I know, so I'll stay here and be an apprentice news hound until I'm all grown up, like fourteen or fifteen." Yulla drew Maru's arm around her shoulders, nestled her head against her chest, and closed her eyes. "I must have early loving and caring, because the Great-Grandmother will pluck me away, hide me all alone in spooky, kooky places, and watch as I try to return on her spiral paths to find the loving and caring again. But if I've had no early loving and caring, I won't know who will truly love and care for me."

# The Carter Chronicles Addendum
## Chronicler
## Dr. Sarah Wessex

In the aftermath of events occurring in the Mexican Sonora during Sarah's month-long absence in Oxford, the news coverage extended beyond fifteen days of fame to a year of headlined incidents. The essence of these various reports will serve to complete the Carter Chronicles. Be alert that Sarah assumed the mantle of a chronicler as a Chamberlain, but she completes it as a Wessex.

### June—Kidnaps in The Despoblado

According to Captain Apache Guardia, a Sonora Federales official, mafioso drug lords fighting for control of smuggling routes across the United States border have kidnapped four Roadways Company executives. No ransom demands have been received thus far, and Guardia fears for their lives. Jorge Catalano and Noah Chamberlain were abducted while surveying a gold deposit in the despoblado. Harold Mason and Roland Zain disappeared while in the region trying to mediate the Cíbola mine shutdown dispute with various warring factions.

### Josiah Chamberlain Demoted

According to Ludie Carter, Roadways president, the long-time managing director has been dispatched to Mexico to concentrate on an urgent new business initiative. He will report to Victor Emblema, president of Emblema Compañia. Chamberlain will undertake an immediate, comprehensive countrywide survey of underdeveloped, sparsely occupied areas lacking roadways. Ludie Carter states that all possible Roadways' resources have been focused on this project. Some sources speculate that Chamberlain is actually spearheading a private search for his son, Noah.

July            ........................................................................

**Sonora Drug War Fails.** Captain Guardia has been reassigned to desk duties in Mexico City, his much-touted campaign against coyote smugglers of drugs and migrants in the Sonora producing no results whatsoever. All suspects residing at the now-defunct Libertad shrine site drifted away into the despoblado once they were deprived of water. Guardia's replacement has yet to be named by Federales officials.

August          ........................................................................

**Kidnappings Debunked.** Mexican authorities have determined that, in fact, no kidnappings of Roadways executives have occurred. Officials contend that Roland Zain caused Harold Mason's death, and inadvertently his own, by a massive explosion in order to eliminate his chief rival for a Roadways top corporate position. Jorge Catalano and Noah Chamberlain were reportedly captured and killed by drug smugglers defending a favored route across the despoblado. Victor Emblema cooperated fully in the investigations and concurs with the conclusions reached. In a related matter, Tomas Mechanico has been acquitted of murder charges associated with the massive explosion at Cíbola mesa last May.

September ........................................................................

**Tres Rios Escuela Honored.** The Mexican Human Development Agency has awarded their prestigious merit of honor to a promising new educational approach developed at a private school in a remote area in central Mexico. Founders, Pepe Tendoy and Cedric Wessex use Spanish-English language instruction and vocational skills building in a synergistic way to prepare Mexican citizens to compete for jobs on both sides of the Mexican border, as well as in Canada. Victor Emblema nominated the school for the highly-coveted award. He has released Josiah Chamberlain for assignment outside of Mexico.

October ........................................................................

**Great-Grandmother Reservation Status Approved.** One million acres, including and surrounding the former Cíbola mesa gold mine, have been set aside for a reservation for Papagos residing in the Mexican Sonora. The original inhabitants of the mesa have been accorded preferential status for homes atop the mesa. The Don Carlos Trust Fund has been established by the Emblema Compañia to ensure the development of housing and schooling facilities and the repair of environmental damage.

November ........................................................................

**Miracle Worker Quarantined.** Maru, leader of the women's movement resulting in reservation status for the Papagos, has been restricted to the Great-Grandmother mesa. Tomas Mechanico and his wife and daughter,

Habita and Yulla, have declined reservation status and moved to Tres Rios in central Mexico.

**Gold Cache Discovered.** Victor Emblema has revealed that the Don Carlos Trust Fund has been enriched by about five million dollars by the discovery of a cache of raw gold in the lower bunker in the pit of the former Cíbola mesa gold mine. Amazingly, he credits young Yulla Mechanico for revealing the whereabouts of the precious metal believed to be the proceeds of Harold Mason's plot to defraud gold from the Emblema Compañia.

December ..............................................................

**Imuris Shrine Site Thrives.** A newly developed shrine site by a spring near Imuris is receiving broad attention and increasing attendance. Nita of Imuris, a leading figure in the recent miraculous reappearance of the Birth Spring on the Great-Grandmother Mesa, is the driving force behind the shrines site's popularity. Fatima, a diminutive, dynamic, folklorica dancer leads her troupe in dances honoring the divine powers of the spring waters, which are enjoying brisk sales in small vials. Performances are noted for their high moral and spiritual content. Gabriel, a featured dancer married to Fatima, plays a larger-than-life masked god of healing with increasing power and poise.

January ..............................................................

**Roadways Acquires Mason.** Carter Roadways Company of Chapel Hill, North Carolina, has acquired controlling interest in the Mason Company headquartered in Toronto, Canada. The acquisition will make Roadways a leading player in the road construction, and reconstruction, boom underway in the United States, Canada, and Mexico. The Mason name will be retired and the enlarged corporate entity will continue to be headquartered in Chapel Hill.

February
....................................................................

**Roadways Awarded Mexican Projects.** Roadways Company, a major force in the North American road construction industry, is the successful bidder for a dozen new road construction projects designed to increase access to some of Mexico's most inaccessible mountainous regions. Major competitors believe the low bids Roadways submitted to secure the new business will prove to be a strategic error for Ludie Carter, president of the rapidly expanding company.

March
....................................................................

**Tres Rios Escuela Awarded Grant.** The Mexican Human Development Agency awarded Tres Rios Escuela twenty million dollars to inaugurate eight additional bilingual vocational learning centers throughout Mexico. Dr. Sarah Wessex has been appointed executive director of the expansion project. She will be headquartered at the Tres Rios Escuela to pursue her new career path. Thus far, the Great-Grandmother reservation and Comitán in the State of Chiapas have been selected for new school locations.

April
....................................................................

**Josiah Chamberlain Fired.** Ludie Carter has discharged Chamberlain, once a leading authority on road construction in Latin America, noting that he no longer has the credentials, or the appetite, for the new strategic path Roadways will pursue. He plans to publish a book someday recounting his pioneering contributions to the road construction industry throughout the Americas. Thus far, his efforts consist of frequent meetings with Wayne Coffer and other Roadways veterans to tell, and retell, stories of daring-do when their names had an impact in their chosen profession in the last century.

May

.................................................................

**Ludie Carter Weds Victor Emblema.** The wedding of Carter and Emblema in Monte Carlo unites two major North American firms. Stock market analysts note that the rapidly expanding juggernaut, which will operate under the Carter Roadways Company name, already enjoys a strong position in open-pit mining of precious metals and is the leading contender to build the much anticipated super-highway to Brazil. Carter's father, Walter "Buck" Smith, gave away the bride and noted with satisfaction that the newly integrated firm will be headquartered in Chapel Hill. Following a brief honeymoon, Victor Emblema will accompany Buck Smith on a series of road rally competitions in exotic locations. Ludie Carter will return to her duties as president of Roadways, staying on the path first entered by her Great-Grandmother Mariah.

# Epilogue

In the future big-business Anglo-Saxons will live in a topsy-turvy world. A female Carter leads the mounted vanguard of a dwindling host, searching for greener pastures to plunder in the south while the Wessex, females and males, follow in the dust and the offal of today's business culture. Has Ludie's Great-Grandmother Mariah placed her female descendants on a spiral path leading to the ultimate defeat of bride-captures? Only the Great Mystery Power can know, so enough of the Carter Chronicles. They now fall silent.

Sarah was born to the wrong people, in the wrong place, at the wrong time, and for the wrong reasons. But she is the great-granddaughter of Ethel Wessex – a descendent of Duke Cedric – who joined the Anglo-Saxon migration to the far west only to be captured and placed in the bondage of a plural marriage, not bringing property to a crowded bed chamber, but becoming the property of a male with vainglorious pretensions of sainthood masking his rape. Unhorsed and vastly outnumbered, she fought valiantly to her death. And for good reason, for Earl Ethelred was the taproot of Sarah's family tree.

Now, Sarah is free of the Carter's orbit and will join Cedric Wessex, a scholar who may yet become a warrior, in his maverick search for his own path to loving and caring. She will join him on the path from the lecture hall back to the armory to be a mounted warrior-scholar in the vanguard. Sarah beseeches the Great Mystery Power for a strong heart and the assertiveness to overcome those who oppose her.

May Sarah be happy.
May Sarah be safe.
May Sarah be peaceful.
May Sarah have ease of well-being.

End

# Book Ordering Information

For additional copies of this publication, please contact:

The Chapel Hill Press, Inc.
600 Franklin Square
1829 East Franklin Street
Chapel Hill, NC 27514
(919) 942-8389
(919) 942-2506 (fax)
publisher@chapelhillpress.com

Please enclose $12.95 for each copy ordered, plus $3.00 shipping and handling for the first book and $1.00 for each additional book. NC residents must also include 6% sales tax. Personal checks and major credit cards are welcome. Please complete the form below and return it with your payment or credit card information.

Name: _____

Address: _____

City, State, Zip Code: _____

Phone #:_____


# Copies:_____ @ $12.95: _____

NC Sales Tax (if applicable) @ 6%: _____

Shipping & Handling: _____

Total enclosed: _____


Credit Card Type: _____

Credit Card #:_____ Expiration Date:_____

Signature: _____